TALES OF C
By
Mike Healey

This book is dedicated to my late father - from whom I acquired, at a very early age, the love for a good story

Copyright
Mike Healey has asserted his right under the Copyright, Designs and Patents Act, 1988 to be identified as author of this work

All rights reserved. No part of this publication may be reproduced, stored in a retrieval system, or transmitted, in any form or by any means, electronic, mechanical, photocopying, recording or otherwise without the prior permission of the publisher.

Disclaimer
While most of the locations are real, the characters and the events of these short stories are entirely the product of the author's imagination. Any resemblance to actual persons, living or dead, is entirely coincidental.

© Copyright 2012 - Mike Healey

Tales of Odd
By
Mike Healey

1
The werewolf of Bethnal Green

It's not at all easy to find a pet shop that sells werewolves, even in London's Bethnal Green.

Chas had been walking for hours, trying every pet shop within a five-mile radius of his council flat. The dingy shop off Sidney Street, badly in need of a lick of paint, was his last chance.

'Do you sell werewolves?' he asked.
'Maybe. Who's asking?'
'I am. How much?'
'Pups is fifteen quid each but a fully-grown one will cost yer fifty.'
'Show me.'

The shopkeeper - a tall, thin individual with the look of a cadaver - immediately disappeared through a curtain at the back of the counter. Chas followed.

It took a moment or two to adjust to the darkness but there, before him, in an iron cage at the far end of a room that smelled of dog shit stood the biggest werewolf Chas had ever seen. Mind you, he was no expert but this beast was lean, mean and with enormous red eyes. It turned to look at Chas, bared its fearsome teeth and growled while saliva dribbled obscenely from its yellow fangs.

'Has it got a name?' asked Chas.
'I call him Spook cos he follows yer wiv his eyes in a very spooky way.'
'Does it bite?'
'You bet it does. Nearly took me bloody arm orf last week!'

The shopkeeper raised his left arm to reveal a very grubby bandage covering his hand and wrist.

'Mind you, it's only when he's about to change that he gets nasty. Then you need to watch yer back. Other times, he's as good as gold.'

'I'll take him,' said Chas.
'Giv us yer money and good luck. I think you might need it!'

Chas paid him his fifty quid in crisp pound notes and left the shop, with Spook in tow at the end of a long lead. At first the werewolf pulled in different directions and Chas had to give it one or two hard yanks - just to show it who was boss. After a while, however, it seemed to settle down and trotted along beside him like a well-trained poodle. It looked pleased to be out of that filthy cage and in the fresh air of Bethnal Green.

It was now quite late and all along the Mile End Road shopkeepers were pulling down metal shutters or bolting steel doors.
Being short and fat, Chas's self-esteem was not particularly high at the best of times so it was with some surprise that he now noticed people staring at him. Or were they staring at Spook? Either way, it made a nice change from the hostility he normally encountered, especially from the numerous young thugs that lived hereabouts.

Perhaps now, with a real live werewolf at heel they might give him the respect he deserved.

Chas reached his block of flats, took the lift to the thirty-ninth floor and unlocked the door to his apartment. He immediately let Spook off its lead and watched him as he explored the flat, sniffing at the soiled clothes scattered all over the floor. Spook seemed happy enough with his new home. He even cocked his leg and peed all over the kitchen mat, as if to mark his territory. He then jumped up onto Chas's unmade bed and before you could say 'Transylvania' was fast asleep and snoring loudly, as only werewolves can.

Chas was chuffed to bits with his new pet. Cats are ok but a real werewolf, well - that *is* something else! He lay down on the sofa, shoved a pair of socks into his ears and promptly fell asleep.

He woke early next morning to discover Spook trying to hump his teddy bear. This moth-eaten toy was a relic of happier, childhood times with his Aunt Edna who had brought him up - after his mum unexpectedly took off one night with a haberdasher from Stepney.

'Stop it, yer daft bugger,' said Chas, hurling a shoe at the great werewolf.

The shoe struck the animal on its left ear and for a moment Chas thought it might turn nasty but it didn't. Instead, it gave him a filthy look and skulked off to the kitchen. Chas followed, feeling somewhat ashamed at having struck his new pet, and poured it a large bowl of milk which it lapped contentedly.

Later that morning he took Spook for a walk in Bethnal Green Gardens.

It was a beautiful spring morning and the trees in the park were starting to sprout leaves. There were quite a few people already out and about, mostly on their way to work but there were also a few loiterers - pimps, perverts, drug addicts, pickpockets etc. - all of whom stared in disbelief at the size of Chas's new pet.

As soon as he smelled grass, Spook took an enormous dump - much to Chas's embarrassment.

Now, it's not generally known that werewolf shit is not doglike but consists of large, black pellets - rather like enormous rabbit droppings. True, they smell far worse but at least you can scoop them up easily. This Chas promptly did, using the Tesco bag he had brought for that purpose.

Chas may have been a dysfunctional, unemployed layabout but he always did his bit for the environment.

Having dropped his Tesco bag into the nearest bin, werewolf and master resumed their morning stroll in the park.

Everything was fine until Chas let Spook off its lead. Big mistake!

The great animal immediately took off at astonishing speed, heading straight towards some woman exercising her dachshund. For a moment Chas thought it might attack the old lady but instead it grabbed her dog in its enormous jaws and tossed it high into the air, catching the terrified animal in its mouth as it fell back down to earth

'Spook, stop it!' yelled Chas.

The werewolf at once dropped the dachshund and came to heel, much to Chas's astonishment. Fortunately, the dog was still alive but the old lady had fainted. Chas put Spook back on its lead and left the park as quickly as he could - before the police turned up.

It was now about eleven-thirty so they slipped into The Kings Arms for a swift pint or two - and to avoid the coppers, should they come looking for a short, fat bloke with a dog the size of a tank.

Once this had been Kray territory.

The Kray twins had terrorized this part of the East End for years yet today their old haunts were almost genteel. Bethnal Green was now the preferred location for well-educated, first home buyers or thrusting young entrepreneurs looking for a quick return on their investments. With the London Olympics looming, Whitechapel Road *et environs* was almost fashionable and many of the old bars, pool halls, clubs and cafes that psychopathic Ron and his evil little brother had 'protected' were now posh wine bars, Vietnamese restaurants, Chinese nail parlours or trendy clothes shops.

Fortunately, such improvements had bypassed The Kings Arms for it was still the dingy old Victorian pub it had always been

Chas ordered a pint of Fosters and a large bowl of Guinness for Spook and sat in his favourite corner opposite the telly.

Chas preferred to keep his own company - and now that of Spook, his new friend and ally. Mind you, it was unlikely that any of the regulars would choose to speak to him, not with a bloody great werewolf staring at you with its bloodshot eyes and lethal jaws unfurled. Spook was evidently a sloppy drinker and extremely mistrustful in company so that between each gulp of Guinness it would raise its snout and stare belligerently at those nearest to it - as if challenging them to try and pinch its bowl. None did, not surprisingly - thereby leaving Chas to enjoy his beer unmolested.

Two hours later and several pints the worse for wear, werewolf and master staggered out onto Doveton Street and headed home.

It was on the journey back to Chas's block of flats that he began to wonder about Spook.

Normally, a werewolf exists in human form - until transformed, at the time of a full moon, into the monstrous lupine shape for which they are traditionally famous. But Spook was different. He already was in werewolf form. So what happened when he changed to his *human* form? The shopkeeper had said absolutely nothing about that, other than that Spook could turn nasty at such times. Besides, he rather liked Spook in his present, terrifying form. Having a werewolf as a pet gave him both street credibility and a measure of protection he had never enjoyed before. Could Spook's human form do as much, he wondered.

The answer to these important questions came a few nights later as a moon as large as a double-decker bus rose over the roof-tops of Bethnal Green.

Spook had been behaving very oddly for the last day or so. On Tuesday, for example, he stopped dead in his tracks, keeled over as if pole-axed and lay with his legs in the air, twitching convulsively. This was not the first time this had happened recently and Chas had found that the only way to stop these convulsions was to kick him in the ribs. Spook would then stop, slowly stagger to his feet like a drunk, steady himself then walk on - as if nothing had happened. Very odd!

At night though it was far worse.

It was now Wednesday and the moon, although not yet full, shone over Bethnal Green like a great paper lantern.

That night Spook stood at the window staring out across the moonlit city, howling like the demented creature that it was. Eventually it clambered up onto the bed, lay down, scratched itself, licked its enormous genitals and promptly fell asleep. This was soon followed by loud snores and the most violent twitching - as if it were experiencing a terrifying, werewolf-like dream. It then rolled off the bed, landed in a crumpled heap on the floor, raised itself onto his front paws and staggered round the room, dragging its hind legs behind it. This bizarre movement was accompanied by the most heartbreaking howls Chas had ever heard - so much so that he hid under the bed with his fingers stuck in his ears until the noise stopped and Spook, utterly shattered, curled up in a corner and slept the Sleep of the Damned.

Thursday now and the moon rose in a cloudless sky, its baleful light illuminating the great city spread beneath it like a threadbare carpet.

Chas was now prepared for the worse. He had seen the signs and knew that he was in for a rough night. He therefore armed himself with a baseball bat and crept under the covers next to Spook, half expecting to be eaten alive by morning. Spook, however, seemed calmer than of late and was soon fast asleep. Chas, his heat thumping, lay close to his great pet, breathing in the rank odour of its mangy fur. Soon he too fell asleep - a sleep though of troubled dreams and restlessness; dreams in which the great werewolf transformed itself into a creature of Hulk-like proportions - green, mean and utterly violent.

What actually happened was that in the morning Chas woke up in the arms of a very camp accountant from Peckham.

'Bloody hell!' said Chas as he leapt out of bed. 'Who the fuck are you?'
'I'm Nigel. Please to meet you, I'm sure.'

Nigel, stark naked under the covers, extended a podgy arm as if expecting Chas to kiss his fingers. Chas recoiled with all the repugnance of a true homophobic.

'Where's Spook? What have you done with him, your poof?'
'Charming, I'm sure. I *am* Spook, you twat. I've changed into Nigel the accountant
 from Peckham. Clever, eh?'
'It 'aint clever', said Chas, 'it's diabolical!

Chas grabbed his clothes and ran for safety into the bathroom. He emerged twenty minutes later, drawn by the wonderful smells coming from the kitchen. There, dressed only in a plastic piny, stood Nigel, preparing breakfast.

'Thought you might like something nice to start the day,' said Nigel, placing the biggest fry-up Chas had ever seen on the table in front of him.

'Ta very much,' said Chas, tucking in. So much for homophobia!

Later that morning Nigel borrowed some clothes and went to retrieve his suitcase from the left-luggage office at St. Pancras railway station. He returned, dressed in tight fawn slacks and a yellow, cashmere pullover. Chas was horrified but said nothing. Besides, it was nearly dinner time.

'Ow come you wos in that cage when I bought yer?' asked Chas as he tucked into a delicious, homemade steak-and-kidney pudding with real mashed potatoes and mushy peas.

'Funny you should ask that,' said Nigel. 'Seymour, the bitch, dumped me. I thought he loved me but clearly not.'

At this point tears welled up into Nigel's eyes. He took from his pocket a large silk handkerchief and blew into it noisily.

'Why did he dump you?'
'Couldn't cope with my mood swings.'
'Mood swings?'

'Well, you know what I mean - changing each month from Nigel to werewolf. Last month, the moment I assumed my werewolf form, he tricked me into visiting some horrid pet shop. Then, between the two of them, they shoved me into that filthy cage. That's when I bit the shopkeeper. I hope he dies of rabies, the evil little tart.'

'Blimey' said Chas. 'Some friends! So wot do you do - when you aint a werewolf?'
'I'm a financial adviser to the rich and famous', said Nigel. 'You know - rock stars, thrusting young entrepreneurs, local drag queens, hairdressers.'
'Does it pay well?' asked Chas, his ears pricking up.

'Very!' said Nigel.

Over the next few weeks Chas's normally humdrum life changed dramatically. It began in the flat. For the first few days Nigel worked tirelessly - washing, ironing, scrubbing and polishing until the place shone. He even bought new sheets and pillowcases. Mind you, peach was not exactly Chas's favourite colour but they were very soft and smelled nice. Nigel also transformed the kitchen, from life-threatening tip to something The Naked Chef would have approved of.

These changes also continued outside the flat. For example, they started to frequent trendy wine bars rather than the dodgy pubs the 'old' Chas had preferred. They dined in smart restaurants and Nigel even showed Chas how to hold his knife and fork and select the best wines. Under Nigel's tutelage, Chas began to read books and take *The Guardian*. They even gave dinner parties at the flat. At first Chas was rather shy of Nigel's colourful friends but they all seemed very nice and treated him very affectionately - even if they did call him 'Nigel's bit of rough' behind his back.

And so, as the weeks passed, Chas changed - from unemployed, dysfunctional thug to a smart young man, well dressed and popular amongst his (new) peers. His sex life improved too, although discretion does not permit a more detailed account here. Needless to say, it was all very different from what he was used to but 'when in Rome, why look a gift horse in the mouth, eh?'

Sadly, all good things must come to an end and one night, four weeks later - as a bright, orange moon rose over the rooftops of

Bethnal Green - Nigel's pink, podgy face suddenly split asunder, revealing the horrendously hairy snout of a great, red eyed werewolf.

'Thank gawd for that,' said Chas as he cuddled up to his adorable, much-missed hirsute pet with its fearsome breath and slobbery jowls.

2
Kafka's dream

Gregor was a plumber. He had been a plumber for as long as he could remember. Even as a child he had been fascinated by drains, water pipes and boilers. Whereas most boys want to fly a jet plane, invade Mars or captain the Sparta Prague football team, young Gregor - even at the age of five - merely wanted to bleed every radiator in the house or replace someone's ball cock.

His full name was Wilhelm Edvard Kafka. No one knew exactly why, therefore, he was called Gregor but life is often a mystery, is it not?

Of course young Gregor had always known who Franz Kafka was (what Czech boy does not know that?) but he had never read any of his books - nor did he ever intend to do so. Unlike his famous namesake, he was not even Jewish although it was said that his grandfather may have been. Anyway, Grandpa Kafka had always been considered the black sheep of the family as he had impregnated his cousin when she was only thirteen. They married soon thereafter but then the Great War intervened and the new groom disappeared for four years. When he returned he had only one leg, one eye and an arse full of shrapnel. The marriage lasted thirty-seven acrimonious years - until, it is rumoured, she poisoned him with arsenic extracted from flypaper.

Gregor was a gentle soul, prone to introspection. He was tall, thin, slightly stooped with sandy-coloured hair and a sallow complexion. He was, by nature, a dreamer and even at the age of forty-seven would drift off - sometimes in mid-conversation. His secret dream was to become an actor.

His break came one Spring morning when it was announced in the local paper that the Sarrandov Film Studios - on the outskirts of Prague - were looking for extras to take part in Peter Kleb's prequel to 'Cannibal Vector'- called 'The Hides of March'. Gregor had no idea who any of these people were or what these particular films were about but this was too good a chance to miss. He at once wrote to the film studios, enclosing the only photograph that he could find - a tattered picture of himself holding a large spanner, his clothes covered in grease and an idiotic smile on his grubby face. The studio loved it and immediately summoned him to Prague.

What happened next was not quite how Gregor had imagined his new career would develop. Fame and fortune he knew would take a little time but once he was established and had given up plumbing for the glamorous life of an actor he was confident that these too would quickly accrue. Mind you, he had never acted in his life, not even at school. Amateur dramatics had passed him by and as for applying for work as an extra, this was his first time.
How he imagined he could become an actor overnight was any one's guess but then hope runs eternal, does it not?

He travelled to Prague by train two weeks later. He was very excited as he stepped down onto the platform, clutching his little cardboard suitcase.

He knew Prague quite well and although they had sent him his taxi fare he preferred to save the money and walk to his hotel. It was a cold night and it took far longer than expected to cross town and find it - a somewhat drab little pension off Krokova Street. It smelled of damp and there were cockroaches. He was glad to slip into bed though, even if he had eaten nothing since leaving home early that morning - apart from a salami sandwich that his elderly mother had made for him. He slept well but forgot to set his alarm and was awoken by loud banging on his door at five-thirty the next morning.

'Mr Kafka,' said an angry voice. 'It's your taxi!'

He dressed hurriedly, forgetting to shave and was driven in absolute silence to the Sarrandov Studios, some five miles out of Prague. It was a wet, dreary morning - not quite the weather he had imagined to signal the start of his new, brilliant career. Of course he knew that a non-speaking 'walk-on' was hardly a leading role but the letter had said that his part was 'significant' and 'central to the film' - whatever that meant. Moreover, the money was good - for a start, at least.

They arrived, twenty minutes late, at the entrance to the large complex that was the Sarrandov Studios.

Gregor was, he had to admit, somewhat disappointed by what appeared to be an old army camp stretching out before them. The numerous buildings, some little more than sheds, were shabby and in need of repair. The pavements were cracked and the roads pitted with holes. Some of the larger buildings had great gaps in their plaster and were clearly in need of a coat of paint. In between these buildings there were old cars, rusty equipment and other rubbish, including painted flats and empty wooden crates. It was a mess and hardly the imposing establishment that the coloured brochure, included with his contractual letter, had vividly described.

They stopped eventually outside a long brick building with green doors and a tatty sign that simply said 'Wardrobe'.

Gregor had never been measured before; it was quite a novel experience. His father was said to have been a natty dresser in his youth. The old suits still hanging in the wardrobe back home were now far too small for Gregor - even if his mother had ever allowed him to try them on. His father had died of encephalitis when Gregor was still a baby. Indeed, he had no memory of his father whatsoever - other than the assumption, acquired at a very early age, that he probably smelled of mothballs. Since his mother had never had either the occasion or the money to buy him a suit, Gregor was thrilled now to step into a tweed affair, rather the worse for wear perhaps, but still very nicely cut. It fitted him like a treat and for a minute or two he walked up and down in front of the large mirror, admiring himself - much to the amusement of the effete young man who had dressed him.

An hour later, having tried on numerous shoes, shirts and waistcoats he was escorted across the way to another brick building with green doors - but this time called 'Makeup'.

Although Gregor had absolutely no experience of theatrical makeup and even less idea of what was involved as far as his part was concerned, he was rather surprised when a sour young woman called Klára immediately sat him in what looked like a dentist's chair and started to shave him with a cut-throat razor. True, he had forgotten to shave that morning but there was no need for her to treat him as roughly as she did - leaving him ten minutes later beardless but now covered in little bits of bloodstained tissue paper.

Over coffee - which he had to buy himself from a machine in the corridor - he sat and pondered his day thus far. Firstly, he had no idea what his part in this film was. The studios had refused to send him a script, adding rather darkly that their decision was prompted by 'issues of security' - whatever that meant. Secondly, although he had been promised money - a large amount for a rural plumber, at least - they had not said how long his contract would last. Days? Weeks? Months, even? Whatever it turned out to be, he would need to tell his mother and make arrangements. Back home in his village near Kolin there was Jakub Krenek's blocked drain, Radek's faulty boiler and Verushka's hanging gutter still to fix. When would he have time for any of these, once 'on location'?

Gregor looked up as a number of young actors, dressed in the styles of the 1950s and talking loudly amongst themselves, swept past. They disappeared round a corner, leaving in their wake a brief evocation of theatrical bonhomie and excitement. It was then that Gregor noticed an open door just down from where he sat. He rose, tiptoed along the corridor and, having checked that no one was looking, cautiously peered round the door.

Before him, in a vast sound stage that was as big as an aircraft hanger, was the film set for some new blockbuster movie. Gregor knew this because it said so on a 'No Entry' sign just inside the door. Countless workmen in white overalls were crawling over some enormous wooden structure, to which they were attaching elaborate plasterwork such as cornices, pillars and ornate architraves. Bits of the building were suspended from the roof, hundreds of feet above Gregor's head, while piles of wood, plaster ornaments and other architectural components were neatly stacked on the floor in every part of the studio. It was simply amazing, not least because for the first time that day Gregor had a real sense of excitement and an understanding of the scale of the projects, including his own perhaps, that went on in this otherwise shabby studio film complex. Was it not here in Prague somewhere that Polanski's 'Oliver Twist' had been shot, only months before?

'Mr Kafka? What are you doing? That is no place for you. Come here. We need to finish you off. This way, please.'

The voice was that of a young man with an abrupt manner and a determined air about him. Gregor quickly followed him back down the corridor and into another part of the Makeup department.

Gregor had never thought that he suffered from claustrophobia but as they smeared Vaseline over his face, stuck two straws up his nose and then plastered him all over with thick, evil-smelling latex he began to panic.

For a moment he could not breathe and felt as if he were drowning. So much so that the determined young man had to restrain him by standing behind the dentist's chair and clasping him round the chest with both arms while the silent, white-coated technician applied more latex. Gregor struggled but then realised that he could actually breathe through the straws and through the short tube they had put between his lips. His panic subsided but it was still a most uncomfortable experience and one that he had not expected in a month of Sundays.

If this was acting for the silver screen you could stuff it, was his considered opinion at this early stage of his new career.

Two hours later, after what had felt like two days, they peeled off the dried latex mask and expressed total satisfaction with the outcome, shaking Gregor by the hand and patting him generously on the back as he staggered to his feet. He was given a towel to wipe the Vaseline off his face and a coffee to take the taste of rubber away. For the first time that day he felt appreciated.

In the main reception area he was given a seat and asked to wait while 'they made the necessary arrangements'. These turned out to be an envelope containing thirty thousand zolty in used notes, a 'release' form that he had to sign there and then and a tram ticket to take him back into the centre of Prague.

And that was it! The end of his film career, so it seemed.

On the tram back into town Gregor sat forlornly, counting his money. He was still not sure what had happened to him, least of all that stuff in the Makeup department. The money was great but what would he say to his mother when he got back home tomorrow? Or his neighbours? He had left with such high hopes and here he was, limping back to his village after a film career that had lasted the best part of five hours. Worse still, he had yet to see a camera or the lights and action and other things that he knew took place on a film set. Moreover, the only set he had seen was for someone else's film and even that was only half built and not an actor in sight. He stared out of the tram window at the rain, feeling utterly miserable. Tonight, he decided there and then, he would drown his sorrows.

Much later that day - long after Gregor had got back to his hotel and had lain down on his bed, feeling sad and lonely - the film crew for 'Cannibal Vektor' rolled into town and set up shop on the quayside near the Palackého Bridge. There were about sixty people, preparing for a sequence to be shot that night on the banks of the Vltava. The rain had stopped but it was a raw night, threatening snow. Temperatures had plummeted and the breath of the riggers showed white under the arc lamps positioned along the water's edge. A great jib, to carry the camera, was being erected while others set up monitors and sound equipment. The Continuity Girl and a few other female supernumeraries clustered for warmth around a large gas fire that had been lit close to where the camera was now being loaded. On the road above the cobbled quayside a small crowd had gathered to watch the excitement.

Meanwhile, Gregor rose from his bed, put on his shabby overcoat and left the hotel to find the nearest bar.

He was still bitterly disappointed but at least he had enough money to enjoy his last night in Prague and get well and truly drunk. To that end he entered a bar just down the street from his hotel, ordered a large brown beer - and swallowed it without taking breath. Two more followed in quick succession. Feeling hungry, he then staggered out into the street and hailed a taxi.

Meanwhile, back at the quayside, the camera was being swung out over the water. Two men, perched on seats on either side of the camera itself, were now peering down into the dark, swirling waters of the river. Several arc lights gave the scene an eerie feeling. Others, controlling the weights at the far end of the jib, made adjustments so that the camera, now finely balanced, could swing out high over the stone parapet high above the water. Another man with a tape measure calculated the distance from the camera lens to the water itself while sound technicians checked their earphones or adjusted radio aerials attached to their sound trolleys. Close by there were now parked five police cars (circa 1950), painted black and white. Taped barriers kept the crowd of curious onlookers - now swelling rapidly - from approaching too close.

When the taxi stopped it was nowhere near where Gregor had expected to be. In fact, it was in a part of Prague he had never seen. Here the streets were mean and dark and the houses looming above them shabby and down-at-heel. From a bar across the street a crude neon light cast lurid patterns onto the road while from the basement of the night club itself came the sound of pop music - loud and insistent. It was called 'The Jackdaw'.

Gregor, now very much the worse for wear, staggered out onto the pavement while pulling from his trouser pocket a large wad of notes.
'How much?'

'Nothing. It's free,' said the driver rather unexpectedly.

Gregor watched the departing cab in disbelief, stuffed his cash back into his pocket and moved towards the entrance of the club. He was met by a dark, somewhat sinister man who promptly led him down into the basement while another locked the street door behind them.

'I wonder,' thought Gregor to himself, 'if they serve food?'

On the quayside the director had arrived, together with a small van from which four technicians now removed a body. It was difficult to see it from their position above the quayside, but a buzz of expectation immediately went around the crowd. Some tried to take photographs while others stared, wanting to catch a glimpse of the figure being carried towards the water's edge. On the river itself a rubber dinghy with two divers in it was moving up and down, trying to stay alongside the camera position whilst moving against the stream.

Back in the basement 'nightclub' - somewhere in the slums of Prague, east of the Wilnova Bridge - Gregor was surprised to see not a bar but a large, bare room in which a number of scantily-dressed women were walking up and down, carrying cardboard placards above their heads.

He was immediately reminded of those girls used to indicate the rounds in a boxing match.

When Gregor's eyes adjusted to the dim light in the smoke-filled room he could see that their pathetic little placards showed not numbers but such things as 'Very Clean' or 'You Want Suck? Or 'Spankie, Spankie?' Moreover, as the girls moved around the room they were making lascivious gestures towards him, occasionally exposing their breasts or winking at him in a very provocative manner. They sometimes spoke - but not in Czech. Their pimp, the dark man who had led Gregor down the rickety stairs, was now standing close behind him and as one particular young girl passed by he gave Gregor a gentle shove in the back, by way of encouragement.

The body at the quayside was now clearly visible. It was that of a tall, thin man with sandy-coloured hair and a sallow complexion.

Back at the brothel Gregor panicked, fought his way back up the stairs and rattled at the locked door as if his life depended upon it. The shifty-looking doorman reluctantly unlocked it - but not until Gregor had given him several thousand zolty for his trouble. Gregor fell out onto the pavement, recovered his feet and set off blindly into the night. It had begun to snow.

At the quayside they lowered the dummy into the water and gently manoeuvred it into position. The cameraman, now high above them, adjusted his position while his assistant checked focus. The body - dressed in a shabby tweed suit, white shirt and waistcoat - was now floating on its back.

Its face was that of Gregor Kafka.

The real Kafka was now completely lost. He had sobered up somewhat in the cold night air but he had no idea where he was or how to get back to his hotel. The narrow street he now found himself in was mean and dark and not a taxi in sight - not that they ever frequented this part of Prague. His encounter with the girls in the 'nightclub' had unsettled him. He was not used to women, especially scantily-clad ones. His mother would definitely not approve but then hopefully there was little chance of her finding out. He for one would certainly not tell her. That way at least, his guilty secret would remain his and his alone. He walked on forlornly, the snow sticking to his hair and face.

It was somewhere near the Old Jewish Cemetery, off Brehova Street, that he first became aware that he was being followed.

He was glad to have stumbled into this area for at least he now knew where he was, even if the thought that he was being followed rather frightened him. He had been brought here by his grandfather many years ago, when he was a little boy. All those gravestones leaning at alarming angles! The idea that there were twenty-thousand bodies, piled one on top of the other in that tiny space had alarmed him even then - that, and the lurid stories his grandfather had told him about the giant Golem that was said to haunt these streets.

He quickened his step, heading towards the river - and safety.

'Turn over. Speed. Action!'

The camera on the end of its great jib rose into the night sky then swooped down towards the body floating in the dark, oily waters of the Vltava.

The two men following Gregor caught up with him under the old wall of the Jewish cemetery. They demanded money. When Gregor refused they each drew a knife, threatening him in a language that Gregor took to be Serb. They were now very close to him. He began to shake with fear. When he tried to run, they grabbed him and threw him violently to the pavement.

'Cut!' said the director. 'That's a wrap.'

The camera swooped back to the ground and was dismantled. The dummy was hauled from the water and put back in its van. The great arc lights cut out, plunging the location into semi-darkness. As the crew packed up, the crowd dispersed. It was now three in the morning.

When the police found Gregor two days later he was floating in the river, just a few yards from where the crew had filmed that final sequence. This time, however, there were no lights, cameras or crowds.

3
Fairies at the bottom of my garden

There are fairies at the bottom of my garden. I know because I have seen them with my own eyes. Many times.

They are very small and look like something between a dragonfly and Kylie Minogue, now that her hair is very short and elfin-like. They whiz about like fireflies and glow in the dark. Sometimes, as evening draws in, I peep from my bedroom window and watch them flitting from flower to flower. They are very lively and seem quite mischievous, in a child-like way. My cat is scared of them. Perhaps they bit her once but whenever they appear she scurries off over the wall or comes indoors and hides under my bed.

I first saw them three weeks ago. Mind you, I had had one or two glasses of gin that evening so at first I assumed they were a figment of my old, befuddled brain but when I closed one eye and looked again, there they were - as bold as brass, dashing about my garden as if they owned the place. Cheeky buggers! Of course I told no one. Not that I have many friends now (most of them are dead, poor dears) but even if I did tell the few that are still (mostly) in the land of the living I am sure that they would not believe me. 'Poor old thing,' they would say. 'Batty as a coot, is our Evelyn. Daft as a brush, just like her mother.'

In one sense they are right.

Ever since I had a mild stroke about two years ago I have not really been myself. At seventy-three you start to go a bit wonky anyway and a stroke certainly does not help. I'm mobile enough but now I forget things easily and would easily lose my head if it were not still attached to my poor old body. Why, only yesterday I found myself half way up our street on my way to our local Spar - dressed only in my slippers and dressing gown. I had a nightie on of course but just imagine what the neighbours might have said. Fortunately, I realised my mistake in good time and scuttled back indoors before anyone saw me.

'Oh look,' they would have said, 'there goes batty Evelyn - out and about in her nightie once more. Silly owld bugger!'

Sometimes I stay up at night, just so that I can watch my fairies. They never come out during the day, clearly preferring the dark. I sit at my back bedroom window and peep between the lace curtains to watch them cavorting about. After an hour or so I usually drop off and wake up the next morning stiff as a board, having slept in my arm chair rather than my bed. Still, it's worth it - just to watch the little darlings. So small, so pretty and so very mischievous. Pity my cat has left, though. I suppose they frightened her off, poor thing.

I have lived in this house all my life. In fact, I was born in this very room, seventy-three years ago on the 18th July, 1933. It was not exactly a happy childhood, what with me Dad being such a bastard. He was never violent, mind you but he always did like a bit of skirt.

When he finally left me Mam for some blonde tart from Brampton she took it very badly, silly cow. I suppose she missed him, despite the way he treated her. Me, I was glad to see the back of him, even if it did mean we had to live on benefit. Mother worked as a cleaner but found it very difficult to hold down a job, even one as menial as scrubbing floors. She was always very moody but after Dad left it got worse. Depression, they called it. More like sour grapes if you ask me.

My fairies are very unpredictable. You never know what they will do next.

The other evening two of them started fighting. Yes, actually clawing at each other like demented things. It was quite scary, really. Like little birds fighting over a worm. I tapped loudly on the kitchen window. Startled by the sudden noise, they stopped fighting, stared at me for a split second and then disappeared - as if by magic. I must say I didn't know they could come and go like that. Clever, eh? Wish I was a fairy. I'd love to disappear, especially when me arthritis is giving me jip. Shuffle off this mortal coil. Pop me clogs. Disappear for ever. That would be nice!

I wonder where they disappear to, the little darlings.

I was nineteen when I got pregnant. He was a lovely lad but as soon as I told him he buggered off, just like me Dad. Mind you, these days young girls get pregnant all the time. Why, I've even seen twelve-year-olds at it in our back alleyway, up against the wall. Bold as brass, filthy little cows. In my day if you got caught it was seen as a terrible sin. When me Mam found out she walloped me and sent me off to her sister's in Haydon Bridge. When the baby arrived it was took off me the same day. I never even got a chance to give her a proper name. Poor little 'Tinkerbell'. She will be fifty-four now. I would love to meet her before I die but I can't see that happening, can you?

One night I moved the curtains too quickly and they saw me.

My fairies have very sharp eyes, rather like birds. They suddenly stopped in mid flight, hovered for a few seconds then darted off into the shadows at the far end of my garden. After half an hour they came back. They seemed more curious than afraid. Indeed, one even hovered close to my window and I swear it stared straight at me. It had dark, almost black eyes in a very pretty, oval face. Of course I ducked behind the curtains but I know that it saw me. It hung there for a few seconds then turned and flew into the uppermost branches of my flowering cherry. There it sat, whispering to the others and pointing in my direction.
I quickly closed the curtains and went to bed in an uneasy frame of mind? What if they are malevolent fairies? What if they mean me harm? I slept badly that night and woke up feeling even more troubled. I suffer from depression sometimes. I'm never quite sure what causes it. My doctor prescribes all kinds of things but I usually flush them down the toilet. This time it was different. I felt a deep unease and spent the rest of the day in something of a daze, unable to do anything.

Later I went for a short walk with the intention of buying a few groceries but when I got there I realised I had forgotten my purse. Luckily I had remembered my keys and could get back into the house but even a cup of tea and a rest with me feet up did not improve things.

Mother's dementia had begun like this. I know because I watched her day by day grow more and more depressed. At first she was just occasionally moody but then her mood swings became quite violent. Mind you, she was always cross with me, whatever I did. Me getting pregnant had not helped but now she seemed permanently angry - as if she blamed me for Dad's sudden departure. He had tried it on with me more than once, even when I was still at school. I told him to bugger off but mother was always suspicious. It got so that she trusted no one, not even her only daughter. That was the start. Later it got much worse.

Last night I stood in the garden, in the dark. At first my fairies just hovered in the shadows, flitting about like nervous sparrows when there is a cat about. I kept quite still, gently humming to myself. I'm not sure why I did that. I suppose I thought that it might calm them, like a lullaby. Well, to my surprise it actually worked! One by one they emerged from the trees and bushes and hovered above my head, like a shimmering halo. When they get excited they seem to glow even brighter. One of them flew so close to my face that I could feel the soft breath of its wings, as gentle as a butterfly. It was lovely. I went to bed that night feeling as if I had at last made real contact with my little darlings.

Mother's conversations were often very odd. She had this habit of saying one thing, then repeating it moments later, as if she were telling it for the first time. I teased her about this at first but she had no idea what I was talking about. Sometimes she would repeat an entire conversation. Our neighbours thought she was as daft as a brush - and said so, which did not help. Of course, the doctors were no help either. They only gave her drugs that made her morose and sullen. I tried to cheer her up as best I could but I was now working in our local chip shop most days so that I was not always there to chivvy her when she got really low. Then she would just stare at the gas fire with a vacant look on her face. She would even dribble. I hated that and always left the room when it happened. Stupid old cow! Why did she have to do that?

It took several days before I could entice any of my fairies into the house. Of course I talked to them, as you would a nervous cat, but their language was so strange, so remote that there was no real verbal communication between us. At first they were very anxious, darting in and out of the kitchen door like demented wasps. After a while I just left them to it and sat in my sitting room with a cup of tea. Slowly, cautiously, one by one, they came in - eventually perching on my mantle-piece. They sat very still, staring at me with their little beady eyes. They looked like small porcelain statues. Very pretty, I thought.

Not being able to talk to them was a bit of a problem. I gave them a nice smile and they seemed to relax but one thing I soon learnt about fairies is they get bored very quickly. One even started to pick its nose, dirty little scamp! Two or three of them then started poking about in my drawers and cupboards. Cheeky little buggers! I clapped my hands and they scampered off, like frightened mice.
I suppose they are like magpies; capable of nicking anything that catches their eye. I will need to watch that if I invite them into the house again. Mind you, I love the way they flutter their wings - like humming birds. It's lovely to watch close up - even if their manners leave something to be desired.

Mother got worse and worse over the next few years.

I was now touching thirty - and, I must admit, still man-mad. I suppose she was jealous, even at her age. However, I seldom brought my gentlemen friends home. If I'm honest, I was embarrassed by her increasingly weird behaviour. Besides, I always preferred sex someplace else - so much more exciting, especially if he was married. I was always very discreet, mind you. No need to rock the boat provided he gave me what I wanted. Of course I never married, not after what she had been through with Dad. Still, I had my fun and never got caught out once - not after that first pregnancy, anyway. True, it might have been nice to have settled down and to have had another baby of me own but it never happened. I suppose I never found the right man.

Meanwhile, Mother got more and more violent.

She starting seeing things - her 'Devils', she called them. They seemed to live in the attic and to talk to her, telling her to do wicked things. At first she simply heard them moving about above her head - footsteps and creaking floorboards, that sort of rubbish. Later, usually in the middle of the night, she would hear them whispering amongst themselves - whoever *they* were. Once I even found her trying to hide under the bed - daft old cow! After several months of this nonsense she said that they were now everywhere - even in her bedroom. I knew it was really all inside her stupid old head but it scared me, I must say.

When I eventually dragged her to the hospital in Hexham - with much screaming and shouting, I might add - the doctors said she had schizophrenia.

Over the next few years I visited her whenever I could but after a while I stopped going, largely because she seldom recognised me. I suppose I might have loved her once but this ugly old woman, propped up in a chair at the loony bin, was not my mother any more. She was a complete stranger to me now. When she died in 1976 she was only sixty-three years old. I was, I must admit, glad to see the back of her. At least I have the house to meself.

I am now seventy-three and quite alone - apart from my fairies. Some of them even live in the house although I do have to keep a close eye on them - thieving little buggers! At night they perch on the end of my brass bed, staring at me. God knows what they do once I'm asleep. I'm sure they run riot but they seldom do any real damage, the little darlings.

One night I was lying on my back on me bed, watching them playing round the light like moths, when suddenly seven or eight of them flew down and took hold of my nightdress in their tiny fingers. To my surprise they then lifted me up and held me aloft, some three or four feet above my bed.

After a minute or two they gently lowered me back onto the covers. It was a lovely sensation. I lay there afterwards delirious with happiness.

Now I'm not so sure about them. They seem to be everywhere. I wish I had not let them into the house, even if they are so pretty and keep me amused with their antics. Last night one of the little buggers actually pinched me. Not in a playful way, mind you. Quite hard, like a spiteful child. Why he did that I have no idea. I can see the bruise even now. Of course I took a swipe at him and missed. They are like flies - they seem to have eyes in the back of their heads. Later that evening another one had a go at me but this time I was ready for it and struck it with a rolled-up newspaper. It fell to the floor, stunned.

They might have taken over my house but I'm still boss around here, that's for sure. Mind you, I had better not anger them too much - if only because I still want them to teach me how to fly.

Two days later my wish came true!

I was fast asleep in bed when one of them tickled my nose, to wake me up. When I opened my bleary eyes I could see dozens of them buzzing around the window - the one overlooking the street. They seemed very excited. While I couldn't understand what they were saying it was clear that they wanted me to come to the window. Even as I climbed out of bed twenty or so of them prized open the sash window with their little fingers while others - hovering on tiny, fluorescent wings - eagerly beckoned me closer.

My front bedroom is above the living room which has a bay window. That means that there is a narrow stone balcony outside that window; more like a stone window-box than a balcony but big enough to stand on. Well, I never imagined that one day I would stand on that balcony - in me nightie, at dead of night. What larks! That really would give the neighbours something to talk about.
I climbed through the window and onto the stone balcony. Some of the fairies held onto my nightie to steady me. Slowly, cautiously, I stood up. I could feel the cold stone on my bare feet. It was a lovely night, not too chilly. The moon was out and twenty feet below me the cobbles of our street sparkled in the moonlight.

So, I was going to fly at last! My fairies were going to show me how to fly. How wonderful. Pity that it's the dead of night and no one about to see me. Still, best practice first.

With that Evelyn slowly raised her arms, spreading them like an angel's wings, and boldly stepped out into the void.

4
The girl with green eyes

Christmas drew closer, bringing with it dark nights of sleet and the occasional fall of snow that in Poznan quickly turned to slush.

Marek hated Christmas. With term now drawing to an end he was unable to sit in a warm library every day, reduced instead to wrapping himself in a blanket in his tiny flat and staring at the gas fire, willing it to ignite of its own volition. If the weather was reasonable he would walk the streets of the old town, his shoulders hunched against the cold, drawing a little comfort from the bustle of tourists, shoppers and trades-people going about their business.

It was while staring into a shop window in the ancient city's main square that he first caught sight of the girl who was to change his life for ever.

Suspended in the window of an antique dealer's shop was a golden cherub illuminated by a single spotlight. This small, wooden figure - its wings spread wide - shone against the shop's dark interior. As Marek stared at it, attracted by its tawdry beauty, he became aware of a young woman's reflection in the glass beside his own. She had a very pale face, large dark eyes and black hair cut in a severe, page-boy style. She was slim and dressed in a long, black, fur-trimmed coat.

Marek was at once conscious that she was not looking at the contents of the shop window but at him, something he rather found disturbing. He had an overwhelming desire to turn round to face her but some instinct told him to hold his ground. Instead, he stared back but such was the intensity of her gaze that he was forced, momentarily, to lower his eyes. When he next looked up the reflection was gone. He spun round just in time to see her stepping into a taxi a few yards away. He watched it drive off across the vast cobbled square, leaving him with a curiously empty feeling. That night in bed he fantasized about this strange girl, bringing himself off with his hand. He fell asleep with the girl's reflection swimming before his eyes.

Two days later he saw her again, waiting for a tram.

He was on his way back from the Science Academy where there was a little café that sold coffee and cakes at student prices. He had had lunch there and had then spent most of that afternoon in the library, studying. Now it was dark and he was on his way home, by way of Plac Wielkopolski.

She stood in a pool of light on the far side of the tram track, silhouetted against the street market that filled part of the square. Rows of wooden stalls, covered in ragged canvas, were illuminated by kerosene lamps that spluttered and spat in the night air. In the dark alleyways between the gaudy stalls late shoppers haggled for a kilo of potatoes or a cabbage perhaps. Marek knew at once that she had seen him. For a moment he was unsure what to do but the sudden arrival of a tram on his side of the track decided matters. He would pretend that he too was waiting for a tram. That way, at least, he could remain where he was and observe her.

For a minute or two he momentarily lost sight of the girl - until the battered old tram moved off, disappearing into the streets beyond. He saw at once that the girl had now moved slightly to one side, out of the pool of light. He could barely see her face, except occasionally when she drew upon her cigarette. Her eyes, however, shone brightly even in the gloom.

She was clearly staring at him, but this time in a somewhat bemused manner, her head tilted slightly to one side - as if sizing him up. Did she already know somehow that he was besotted with her? Having hooked her victim, was she now leisurely drawing in her line? Marek, for his part, pretended not to stare, looking casually about him as if unaware of the young woman intently studying his person. For a moment he even began to bask in her attention, luxuriating in the knowledge that at least one woman in Poland patently admired his dark good looks.

This moment of vanity was short-lived for suddenly a blue tram, covered in graffiti, swung into the square and passed between them, screeching to a halt opposite. Marek was at once overwhelmed with panic, unsure whether or not he dared cross the track and follow her onto her tram. This brief hesitation was his undoing for moments later the tram moved off, quickly gathering speed and screeching like a stuck pig as it veered off out of the square.

The area opposite was now full of people who had got off but there was no sign of the girl. Marek was devastated and stamped his feet and waved his arms about like an angry child, attracting the stares of those nearest to him. But then some instinct told him to look up at the retreating tram. There, gazing out of the rear window was the girl. As the tram disappeared into the dark, Marek swore that she waved one hand at him - but slowly, languidly.

Marek wandered back to his flat that night in a daze.

He took his usual, circuitous route, thereby avoiding the open squares and narrow streets of the old part of the city. He found some consolation in the way he successfully negotiated the intricate patterns formed by the cobbles and paving stones across which he stepped, like a child avoiding the cracks. Sometimes, where tramlines criss-crossed the street, he froze with fear - unable to progress beyond such malevolent intricacies.

Although he was a physicist and a mathematician by training, he had always been interested in art. In the geometric paintings of Piet Mondrian, for example, he found regularity and a pictorial clarity - qualities that he had never found in his normal working life. These paintings therefore gave him enormous pleasure and although he could not afford a book about the artist, he did own a postcard reproduction of Mondrian's 'Opposition of Line: Red and Yellow' that somehow calmed him whenever he felt agitated. In the real world, however, a single shattered paving stone in his path would immediately induce panic, forcing him to retrace his steps until an alternative route presented itself.

It was late by the time he reached his street. The ground floor hallway was poorly lit and it was with some difficulty that he groped his way towards the old iron staircase. He grasped the familiar rail with relief and cautiously made his way up the rusty stairs to his tiny flat on the third floor. He carried his key on a string round his neck, withdrew it from beneath his ragged shirt, unlocked the iron door, entered then securely bolted it behind him before collapsing, fully-clothed, onto his bed.

He dreamt that night of the mysterious girl. It was a troubled dream that made little sense, riddled with unrelated anxieties. It consisted largely of a strange journey across the city - a desperate, slow-motion race against time towards some unspecified destination. The girl herself appeared only once, floating upright at the foot of his bed. She wore a thin, white dress. With one hand she held her skirts above her navel, revealing her naked thighs and belly. With the other hand she caressed herself - slowly and with studied deliberation. When Marek woke up there was a wet patch on his sheet and a feeling of utter desperation.

He was aware now that this girl with the green eyes and jet-black hair was slowly, ineluctably taking possession of his lonely life.

For the next three days he hung about the tram station in the hope of seeing her once again but she never reappeared. He cut a sorry figure, even amongst the beggars who frequented the far end of the square. Here there were skips full of refuse from the street market through which these unfortunates scavenged for food. Marek sat forlornly on a bench in the shadows, only dimly aware of the activity of these ragged men and women. Once, a bedraggled old man, dressed in filthy rags, took from the skip several tin cans, placed them on the cobbles and began to jump up and down, crushing them beneath his feet. His dance was crazy, manic and caused passers-by to stare or cross the street to avoid him.

As night drew on, prostitutes gathered in the shadows of the abandoned market stalls, openly soliciting men hurrying home. Every now and then one would stop, agree terms and disappear with his girl behind the awnings of the nearest canvas stall. Marek, blissfully unaware of all this salacious activity, merely stared at the trams coming and going. Marek's girl never reappeared and after a few days he gave up looking for her and instead withdrew to his little flat.
Money was now very short. In previous years his ailing mother had

occasionally sent him a few crowns but that source had dried up as he had long since stopped writing to her. He got a meagre grant from his university but that only just paid for his flat, leaving little for food. He had pawned what few luxury items he had once possessed - such as his watch and transistor radio. Now he had nothing. He was far too insecure to hold down a job, even as a cleaner. He had tried that once but had been defeated by the thousand tiny, malevolent cracks in the lino that covered each dingy corridor.

One evening later that week he entered the café opposite his apartment and purchased a cup of black coffee with the last few coppers still in his pocket. He had one hundred and thirty-two zloty left in a tin hidden under his bed. This would probably feed him for a few more weeks but once that was gone his situation would become truly desperate.

He sipped his coffee slowly, luxuriating in its sickly-sweet taste although conscious that this was an indulgence he could ill afford.

It was some moments before he realised that the girl was actually sitting at the bar, observing him in the large mirror opposite. She was perched upright on her stool, her long legs crossed and one elbow resting casually on the bar top. In her other hand she held a French cigarette, her long red nails clearly visible.

Marek was suffused with joy and anxiety in equal measure. He immediately looked away, staring intently at his half-empty coffee cup but then as quickly looked back - in case he was hallucinating. No, it was not a dream. The girl was still there, bold as brass. Now she was smiling at him through the mirror, occasionally drawing on her cigarette and blowing the smoke towards him in a gently provocative manner. Marek stared back, unsure whether to smile or not. Her eyes were truly green - dark, lustrous, like the sea. Even in the dim light of the café her pale face appeared almost white while her mouth was a precisely defined area of intense red. Marek's head began to swim. He looked down and stirred the sediment at the bottom of his cup, noticing that his hand was now shaking, causing his spoon to rattle against the rim of cup.

When he next looked up the girl had vanished, leaving only a smouldering cigarette in the ashtray on the bar.

Marek found it hard to explain his feelings. Alone that night in his little flat he was consumed with anger; anger that she should vanish before he had had a chance to speak to her or establish some sort of relationship, no matter how tentative. Perhaps she was some kind of high-class prostitute, touting for custom? Or perhaps she was just a well-paid office girl who had taken pity on a lonely, impoverished scholar. Did she despise him for his hangdog looks, the result only of low self-esteem and poverty?

Marek was a brilliant scholar. He had been top of his year at the university in Poznan and a mathematician who, during his brief tenure with Professor Piotr Pieranski, had grappled, no less, with computerised ways of creating a true Gordian knot. He had helped devise the SONO programme, itself predicated on the notion that matter is made up of tightly coiled (perhaps knotted) loops of space time. Even now, amidst all this emotional confusion and anxiety, he was working on theories related to topological quantum computing, using anyons - bizarre, particle-like structures that are possible in a two-dimensional world. The walls of his room were covered with mathematical formulae that proved, or so he hoped, that topological properties are unchanged by small perturbations. Like the Gordian project, this work involved quantum knots. Were these not achievements to be valued, even by this strange, mysterious girl?

That night, in his dream, he raped her.

They were in the library. He forced her back across a table, pulled her knickers to one side and entered her brutally. Their violent struggle sent books and lamps crashing to the floor. She resisted valiantly but he was far too strong. When he eventually climaxed the small audience of scholars and librarians who had gathered to watch his triumph applauded loudly.
Marek awoke the next morning, rose from his bed and staggered to the window, parting the dusty net curtains with one hand. The café where he had almost spoken to the girl was clearly visible across the street. In the cold light of day it appeared shabby and in need of

a fresh coat of paint. Its neon signs, once vibrant flashes of colour in the night, were now twisted worms of dull, tubular glass. Inside, an old woman mopped the floor while the barman morosely polished glasses, a cigarette hanging from one corner of his mouth.

Marek closed the curtains and went back to bed and tried not to think of the girl with green eyes.

He must have fallen asleep eventually for he dreamed that he was in a tower overlooking the old town square. Far below him were rows of Renaissance houses, each one a different pastel colour. The square itself was empty, its wet cobbles shining in the light of a row of Art Nouveau street lamps. In the centre of the square a stone statue depicted a naked girl writhing in the arms of a satyr. Suddenly Marek stepped off the balcony and hung, suspended, above the square - like a wingless angel.

It was at that point that he awoke with a start.

At noon Marek got out of bed and washed himself, meticulously scrubbing his hands until they almost bled. He got dressed (slowly) and when ready retrieved his little tin of money from under the bed, removing a few coins before carefully replacing it. He made his way down the old iron staircase, ritually touching every third upright. He then crossed the shabby, ill-lit lobby and left the building, his heart beating faster and faster. After a moment's hesitation at the kerb, alarmed at a dislodged manhole, he took a deep breath and boldly crossed the street. Breathless, his heart pounding wildly, he entered the café.

She was not there - much to his relief. At least he could now arrange himself, gather his thoughts and await her arrival - with equanimity. Of course he had no idea whether or not she would come again but for those in love, hope springs eternal. That Marek was in love there was no doubt. True, he had had little success with women hitherto. Indeed, he was twenty-three and still a virgin but at least he had now found someone interested in *him*. This was an entirely novel experience and an opportunity that he must not let slip, certainly not through shyness or lack of determination...

He ordered his coffee. When the barman placed it on his table he meticulously rearranged his cup and saucer, putting the spoon neatly to one side and making the lumps of sugar into a tiny, pyramid-like stack. He knew this time, moreover, that he had sufficient money in his pocket to offer the girl with green eyes a drink - provided she stuck to a glass of cheap wine or an ordinary coffee. This gave him a confidence that now suffused his body with a warm, unfamiliar glow. For the first time for weeks he felt happy and self-assured.

Could this be the start of something new, some close relationship, even love that would change his miserable life for ever?

She appeared, as if on cue, twenty minutes later and sat at the bar exactly as before. If she saw Marek she certainly did not acknowledge him - not even with a knowing glance or a brief smile. She ordered a glass of wine, arranged her hair in the mirror then lit a Gitane. Marek, assuming the manner of one entirely unaware of her presence only a few feet away from where he sat, nonchantly sipped the remains of his cold coffee. Every now and then he would surreptitiously look in her direction or sneak a glance in the mirror. She, for her part, resolutely refused to even glance at him. He was glad, however, that there was no one else in the cafe to catch her attention or distract her from him.

She was truly beautiful, dressed as she was in a short dress of black silk. She wore black, high-heeled shoes and stockings that gave off a dark, silvery sheen. Her face, still deathly pale, was beautifully composed - even if she still refused to acknowledge the physical presence of the young man so patently, so desperately in love with her luminous beauty and lustrous green eyes.
What happened next, however, rapidly acquired the character of a dream, for nothing that took place thereafter was on rational grounds remotely explicable.

The girl slipped from her stool and - to Marek's utter astonishment - crossed to where he was sitting, bent over and gently kissed him on the neck. Marek, whose head now swum with a delirium he could hardly contain, was aware only of her perfume and the warm touch of her lips. Before he could respond she took him gently by the sleeve and led him out of the café - watched in utter astonishment by the barman. They ended up in the darkened alley at the side of the building. Here, amidst the dustbins and crates of empty beer bottles, she drew him close to her, kissing him long and hard on the mouth.

Marek's excitement at this unexpected turn of events was short-lived. Even as his body responded to her kisses his hands closed about her neck, grasping her firmly by the throat. She struggled but it was useless. Within minutes she lay dead at his feet, her crumpled body sprawled on the cobbles. Marek stepped back, gazed in horror at what he had done then ran off down the alleyway, across the deserted street and into his apartment block. When he paused for breath in the shadows at the foot of the rusty old iron staircase his heart was pounding and his hands were wet with fear. He then returned to his little room, locking the door securely behind him.

He sat on his bed and held his head in his hands - riddled with guilt and shame. There were tears in his eyes and a sick feeling in his stomach.

To have killed the one thing he loved was absolutely monstrous. He was - like his hero Raskolnikov, in Dostoyevsky's 'Crime and Punishment' - now utterly consumed with guilt. To have done that to someone who might even have loved him, who certainly desired him, was odd beyond belief. Besides, it was not in his character to be violent. True, he could be obsessive - he knew that. But that was something he could control by ritual, by his strict routines and self-imposed disciplines. What therefore could have possessed him this time? All that he knew now was that he was a monster and would surely be punished for such a hideous crime.

That night he dreamt that the beautiful girl with green eyes hung from his ceiling like a crouching panther, ready to drop upon him the moment he closed his eyes. Eventually, overcome with mental and physical exhaustion, the vision vanished and he fell into a deep, merciful sleep.

Early the following morning Marek rose from his bed and crept to the window. He cautiously parted the net curtains, quite expecting to see police outside the café or even surrounding his apartment block but the street and the alley beside the café were completely empty. Indeed, there were not even those red and white tapes used by police to protect the crime-scene. Nothing, in fact, to suggest that anything out of the ordinary had taken place that night. And what of the café staff? Had not the barman at least seen him leaving the bar with the girl? Could he have failed to report that to the police? Surely not. Her murder had been real enough but then perhaps someone had removed the body. It was all very confusing.

Marek stayed in his room for the next three days, regularly checking the street below for police activity. There was none. Desperate now for food, he left the flat late one night, nervously crossed the street to the café and peered in through its window. It had been raining all that day and the glass was streaked with grime. Inside the barman had lit candles as usual, giving the shabby interior a certain atmospheric, albeit greasy charm.

To Marek's utter astonishment there, seated exactly as before, was the girl - even then lighting a Gitane.

Naturally, his heart skipped a beat or two but so pleased was he to see her alive and well that he immediately entered the café and crossed to where she sat. Silently, like long-lost lovers, they embraced.

Later that night, in a dark alleyway behind the zoological gardens, Marek stabbed her to death with a scalpel he had stolen from work.

5
Rites of Passage

The last time I saw Harry he had a glass eye and was accompanied by a very large albino Alsatian. He had always needed protection of one sort or another - he was, after all, a villain - but how he came to actually lose that eye is another story altogether.

It all began in the summer of 1961. We worked at the Cavendish Arms, a large roadhouse on the Thanet Way. It was a place where coaches stopped on their journey to and from Herne Bay or Margate. It was a bit rough at times; well, boisterous is perhaps a better way of putting it. A coach-load of weekend trippers from London's East End hell-bent on having a good time and getting tanked up in the process was what we had to deal with - several times a day. Mind you, we were good. There were only five of us - four behind the bar and Paulo in the kitchen - but if two coaches turned up simultaneously we could serve forty-five double gin-and-tonics, thirty pints of Bishop's Finger and twenty Port-and-lemon in ten minutes flat.

Harry was not really one of our regular customers but he often dropped in on his way to work.

He drove a silver Jaguar of which he was inordinately proud. Once he took three of us for a spin - up and down the dual carriage way for a mile or so, doing a ton there and back. I had never been so fast in my life but Harry was a good driver and he had never been stopped by the police. He was a tall, slim, handsome man in his late thirties with long, silvery-blond hair that made him look more like an actor than a crook. The girls thought he was dishy but we were less sure. Of course, he was something of a ladies man and had tried it on with Rebecca but she was having none of it. Still, after her polite but firm rebuff he still treated her like the rest of us - with rather old-fashioned courtesy, even though we were students.

We worked long hours at the pub but this was a summer job and we all needed the money so no one ever complained. The boss and his alcoholic wife usually left us alone. They too seemed to like us, probably because we were the first bar-staff they had ever had who did not rob them blind. Besides, we were a young, lively bunch and always got on well with the customers - even when they got drunk and started throwing glasses at each other.

Anne, who was the quiet one amongst us, usually dealt with any rowdy customers. She had a wonderful smile and a gentle way of defusing ugly situations. No lad likes to be scolded by a winsome flower-child in Laura Ashley smock and sandals but Anne always got away with it. It was magic to watch. Often the other customers would applaud as she quietly walked back to the bar, leaving two wild lads - now as good as gold, mind you - with red faces, ruefully sipping their beers.

Paulo was the eldest. He was in his third year at college. Although a brilliant graphic designer he never talked about college work and was seldom seen to open the numerous sketch books he kept at his bedside.

His passion, however, was cooking and every year, for the last four summers, he had worked as Head Chef at the Cavendish Arms. It was thanks to him that we all got the job in the first place - even though I had to lie about my age.

Mind you, Paulo was something of a tyrant in the kitchen and gave the other staff a hard time. We were never allowed anywhere near his domain, even for a sandwich. But his food was great and the restaurant was always full. His clientele were a lot better than ours - commercial travellers, local business men and their like. It was two, completely separate worlds divided only by a wall and yet he was king of his and we were lords of ours. Funny that. I was still a schoolboy and rather naïve I suppose but that pub taught me something about class that my school never did. Them and us, that's how it was.

That's why I decided, at the ripe old age of seventeen, that I would become one of 'them' - and that's where Harry came in.

Harry ruled the roost in Faversham and beyond. His territory stretched all round the Kent coast - from the Isle of Sheppey to

Whitstable, Herne Bay, Margate and Broadstairs. Where ever there were whelk and cockle stalls Harry was 'the governor'. Not that he actually owned any such stalls but he did 'protect' them. In other words, if the stall-keepers did not pay Harry they would find their little stalls floating in the harbour at dawn the following day. Sometimes, if they still refused his 'protection', one of his thugs would teach them a lesson they would not forget. Of course Harry never told us any of this; we found this out from the lads at his local in Faversham. Here they spoke of Harry in hushed, respectful tones - just in case he dropped in for a swift half or one of his mates reported it to the 'governor'.

We lived next door to the pub, just a mile or two from where we worked. It was a shabby stone cottage with a thatched roof but we loved it. It had three bedrooms - one for the girls, one for Paulo and one which I shared with Nick. Very cosy. Sometimes we lit a fire and sat on the battered sofas in front of the great hearth, illuminated only by the flames, sipping cider. Of course, being students we spent most of the evening putting the world to rights - or slagging off our tutors. The girls and Nick were second year art students in Canterbury but I had only just left the sixth form at Simon Langton's Grammar School. If my grades were ok I was destined for Oxford later that year. This still made me the baby of the team. However, they treated me well enough, even though I must have appeared very unworldly to them.
Not surprisingly, the sleeping arrangements described above changed as the summer progressed.

Nick moved into Paulo's bed, leaving me on my own but yearning to be in Anne's bed next door. Rebecca, who only had eyes for Nick, sulked for weeks when he ended up in Paulo's arms rather than hers. This made it very hard for Anne who did not want to sleep with anyone - least of all me. Like me she was still a virgin and determined to stay that way - until she met 'him'. None of us were sure who 'him' might be but for a flower-child of the Sixties Anne was remarkably old fashioned. Paulo was convinced that 'he' would be a rich stockbroker or, worse still, her favourite (married) lecturer with whom she already flirted at every opportunity.

As for me, well I had no chance so it seemed and therefore spent lonely nights in my little bed thinking of Anne in hers. Only Paulo, who could be very moody, liked the new arrangements and under Nick's genial, easygoing influence, even he mellowed. We were, therefore, a very happy little family - despite the odd sexual tensions prompted, occasionally, by too much cider.

It was a brilliant summer that year. We arrived early, in time to see the late apple blossom burst on the scene, turning the orchard behind the Cavendish Arms into a sea of white foam, flecked with pink and green. One evening, on our day off, Anne made us all lie in a circle on the grass with our heads close to the trunk of a particularly splendid tree. With arms outstretched and our fingers touching those of the person on either side, we encircled the tree like a human 'mandala' - well, that's what Anne said. Me, I just loved the feel of the grass beneath me and the sunlight flickering between the leaves above, casting dappled shadows. I didn't get to touch Anne's fingers but on the way back to the cottage I told her how much I had liked her idea and was rewarded with a ravishing smile.

Harry popped in to the Cavendish the following day - for a beef sandwich and a pint of Shepherd Neame's best bitter.

He was in a good mood - flirting with the girls and chatting openly to us about his ex wife Vanessa and their daughter 'Butch'. It seems that he and Vanessa had separated three years ago. Vanessa had a new lover called Brian whom Harry thought looked a bit like Hugh Paddick from 'Beyond Our Ken' - roll neck sweaters in pale pastel colours and sleeked-back hair. Harry thought Brian might actually be gay but he and Vanessa seemed happy enough in the sack - if you know what I mean.

At this point Harry leered at Rebecca but she went on polishing glasses and refused to be drawn into the conversation

Harry also had a new partner - Geraldine. Geraldine was a brassy young blonde with a really fabulous figure and the attention span of a goldfish - well, that's how Harry described her and who were we to argue? Disagree with Harry and you could end up in the boot of his Jag with a dagger between your ribs (Anyway, that's what Nick said).

Me, I just loved the way Harry talked so freely about his domestic arrangements. I had no idea why he trusted us with his secrets. Perhaps it was because we were students and as far removed from his world as you could get or perhaps because we were genuinely interested and quite without ulterior motives. What we all found fascinating, however, was that Harry, Vanessa, Brian, Geraldine and seven-year-old 'Butch' all lived together in the same palatial, mock-Elizabethan mansion on the outskirts of Faversham.

'Come and have a drink one evening,' said Harry, as he supped up and left. 'I'll tell Geraldine to make us something to eat.' We could hardly wait.

Life in a big pub is not all beer and skittles. That night a fight broke out between a bunch of London taxi drivers and some local farming lads. The Londoners were mostly Jewish so I suppose it was only a matter of time before someone said something untoward.

The trippers had called in to the Cavendish Arms on their way to Margate for a liquid lunch. Two hours later they were ready for a sleep on the beach. Now, on their way back home, they called in for another drink - or three!

I'm not sure who threw the first punch but within minutes there were seven or eight grown men smashing each other over the head with beer bottles - cheered on by their womenfolk. In the confusion we forgot to turn off the jukebox and the whole fight was accompanied by Don Gibson's 1958 recording of 'Oh, Lonesome Me'. Very surreal!

When the police eventually arrived there was blood all over the floor and several men out cold on the soggy carpet. Anne and Rebecca were in tears and hiding in the back room. A number of arrests were made while the boss, Nick, Paulo and I attended the wounded. That evening, as we walked back to the cottage, we were strangely silent. It had been an ugly scene and we were still quite shaken. Not even the intoxicating scent of the lilac draped over the entrance to our little cottage could calm our shattered nerves. Mind you, it was not the first time there had been violence at that pub but it was still shocking to experience it at close hand.

None of us slept much that night - not least me.

Sometime around one in the morning there was a timid knock on my bedroom door. It was Anne. She was wearing a long, white Victorian nightdress and looked ravishing in the moonlight pouring in from my open window. I held the covers back and she slipped into bed. She was trembling. We lay there, just holding each other. I'm not sure if either of us slept well that night but I certainly woke up at dawn with this lovely girl still in my arms. When she finally opened her eyes she seemed none the worse for her night in my bed and appeared to have forgotten the fight from the night before. When she left to return to her room (before Rebecca woke up) she kissed me lightly on the lips. I spent the rest of the day in a daze - and with an excruciating pain in my groin.

Harry's 'business' had its ups and downs too.

Sometimes he would drop in for a drink and not say a word, staring morosely into his double 'Bloody Mary'. Other times he would be the life-and-soul of the party, chatting with the transient customers as if they were old friends. He was a real raconteur, despite his lack of education. I suppose we must have seemed very middle-class and well educated in comparison to him. I must confess I had never thought of such things until I met him but then my life seemed very dull when compared to the exciting, albeit brutal one that he clearly lead.

He was, after all, a violent criminal - therein lay his appeal to us, I guess.

Harry did not like eating in the restaurant so Paulo would occasionally cook him something special, which he would eat seated at our bar. Then, after consuming the larger part of a bottle of our best red wine, he would tell us of his childhood - skiving off school to work in the hop fields or running wild over the mud flats on the Isle of Sheppey.

Occasionally, he would talk about the step-father who beat him - until the day he was big enough to fight back. Some say he killed the man but Harry never told us what really happened and none of us ever had the bottle to ask him.

Summer drew on, the blossom vanished and the fruit began to appear in the lovely orchards that surrounded the pub. Nick said we lived in a world not unlike that of Samuel Palmer's idyllic Shoreham - with its fleecy sheep and ripe cornfields bathed in refulgent gold. I told him he was an incurable Romantic. Besides, I had no idea who Samuel Palmer was and, moreover, had no interest in finding out. But he was right in one respect. That summer was truly wonderful, what with long walks in the moonlight, good conversation and the heavy scent of newly-cut grass filling the evening air as we walked the mile or two back to our cottage.

Since Monday was our day off we took to long rambles in the afternoon. Paulo would conjure up a delicious picnic while Nick planned our route. Not that it mattered where we went, as long as we ended up somewhere nice for lunch - preferably by a stream or in a bluebell wood. After a while the Fine Artists amongst us became quite fussy and anything less than 'stunning' was soundly rejected. As for me, well as long as I was near Anne I did not care where we were. True, nothing much had happened since our night together but she occasionally linked arms with me as we made our way back to the cottage, the air filled with the heady scent of wild rose and lilac from the hedges lining the little lane in which we lived. That brief touch from Anne was enough to make my day and I went to bed each night with a beating heart and a head filled with wild fantasies, some of them quite rude.

The trip to Harry's Faversham mansion finally arrived and in our best bibs-and-tuckers we crowded into a taxi and headed for 'Belvedere Hall'.

Vanessa proved to be a voluptuous brunette with an engaging smile and a wicked sense of humour. Brian too was something of a surprise; a more polite, urbane man one could not imagine. Geraldine was exactly as Harry had described her but turned out to have studied law at St. Hilda's College, Oxford - Harry had forgotten to mention that bit. Harry was Harry and pleased as punch to see us, ushering us into a large sitting room that reminded Anne of

Liberty's Regent Street emporium. There were expensive Persian carpets on the floor but a hideous, fake Venetian chandelier above. The room was littered with very modern chairs and sofas covered in rather dubious 'leather'. While everything was clearly very expensive, nothing matched and I saw the fastidious Paulo visibly wince as Harry proudly showed us round his 'stately home'.

I cannot recall much of the rest of the evening - what with the generous quantities of fine wine Harry poured down our throats and the splendid cold buffet Geraldine supplied - even Paulo was impressed. He and Geraldine accordingly spent a large part of the meal swapping recipes. After supper we rolled back the expensive carpet, put on the EP player and danced the night away. Harry danced a lot with Rebecca but no one seemed to mind, least of all Geraldine who had rather taken a fancy to me.

When the marihuana miraculously appeared the evening descended into a kind of fog through which I, who had never smoked dope in my life, serenely floated. Even Anne, who had always disapproved of drugs, joined in, dancing by herself in one corner of the room in a slow, trancelike state - all very 60's. As for me, well, I was in seventh heaven, what with the soporific effect of the marihuana itself and the warm glow of too much red wine in my bloodstream. However, as I drifted, as it were, across the ceiling - held aloft by squeals of laughter from Rebecca who, when drunk, always became wildly hysterical - I became dimly aware of the sharp, disapproving stare of a little girl on the landing, wearing a winceyette nightdress and clutching a teddy-bear by its leg. That must have been 'Butch'.

Summer was now drawing to a close and our time at the Cavendish Arms was about to end. Soon we would go our separate ways. Although we each promised to keep in touch I knew that I would probably not see any of them ever again. My family were leaving Canterbury and moving to The Lake District and I was off to university. Worse still, I had made little progress with Anne and now played Don Gibson on the jukebox several times a day - much to the annoyance of the others.

In those remaining days we did not see much of Harry - or his extraordinary *ménage* at Belvedere Hall.

There was talk of trouble with rival gangs now operating the east coast. Rumour had it that the police were closing in, having for years turned a blind eye to Harry's nefarious ways. Of course, many of these same policemen had been on the take but now, with others vying for his patch, Harry was in trouble. Sporadic fights had broken out between Harry's men and those of rival gangs, outsiders from south London. Pickings were rich and for years Harry had had the spoils all to himself. Now others wanted a share and were prepared to go to any lengths to get it.

We of course knew very little of these ourselves but the town was rife with rumours, some of them very ugly indeed.

Things came to a head on our last night at the Cavendish Arms.

It began with some of Harry's men meeting for a quiet drink in their local pub in Faversham itself, next to our cottage. There were a number of unfamiliar faces in the bar that night but none of Harry's men were overly concerned. They were, after all, on their patch. This was their pub and what they said, went.

Harry himself arrived late but in time to break up an argument between one of his bodyguards and a strapping young lad from Rainham. No one can remember what they were arguing about - football, probably, but it had quickly turned nasty. Harry managed to pull the two men apart, trying to defuse the situation with a joke but it was a set-up and immediately other strangers (rival gangsters) joined in. Within minutes the argument had escalated into a full-scale battle, with knives and cudgels. No one is sure who rang for the police but they arrived promptly - too promptly, some said. With truncheons drawn, they waded in. In the mayhem that followed, several gangsters were cudgelled to the ground, some escaped while others were overwhelmed, handcuffed and bundled into police vans.

Harry, whom the police had clearly targeted, was one of the first to be restrained. He was on his knees, hands manacled behind his back and blood pouring from a knife wound on his neck when one of the rival gang broke free from his captors and took a final swing at a defenceless Harry.

The local hospital had to deal with the aftermath. Apart from superficial cuts and bruises there were three cases of concussion and no less than seven men with serious knife wounds, including Harry. They stitched Harry up but were unable to save his right eye.

Our last night in the cottage, next to where the battle had taken place earlier that evening, was very quiet. No one felt like celebrating - not when our landlord told us in detail what had happened. Rebecca wanted to visit Harry but it was said that he had been arrested and taken directly from the hospital to the remand prison in Maidstone. Mind you, the Kent police had been after him for years so perhaps this was all the excuse they needed to bang him up.

We packed, ready for departure early the following morning, and went to bed. I hoped Anne would join me but she never did so I spent my last night in our little cottage all by myself - 'Oh lonesome me'. No change there but something had changed in me, leaving a sour taste to an otherwise idyllic summer.

Harry was released five years later, by which time I had graduated and was trying to hold down a job in a small theatre in Canterbury. I recognised him at once, even though he was on the other side of the street. He had an enormous dog at his side - a strange, white creature. Harry had aged but was still the handsome, striking figure I remembered.

I did not cross the street to say hello and I doubt if he saw me, what with his glass eye and all. Anyway, I hope not.

6
Love is blind

Who would have thought that one spring morning a thirty-foot mechanical doll would wake up and attempt to escape, or so it seemed, through the streets of London? But sure enough, that is exactly what happened - with dire consequences for all concerned, especially Sid.

The Mayor of London, with whom the buck normally stops, refused to accept blame for what, after all, began as mere street theatre. The German company, commissioned to create a giant elephant and an enormous latex child on a tricycle, were equally blameless - or so the Coroner subsequently claimed.

It all began with a parade - watched by large crowds, most of whom were astonished that morning to round a corner near Admiralty Arch and be confronted by a massive elephant squirting water at anyone who ventured close. The elephant - made of reinforced latex with articulated, mechanical legs and animated trunk - stood nearly forty-feet tall, with ears the size of a small terraced house. On its sides and back it carried ornate Indian structures on which stood four or five operators, dressed in elegant oriental costumes.

The child, however, was constructed differently, with four outriders perched on elevated seats with pedal contraptions which provided motive power. Each operator was dressed as a flunky - in satin breeches, silk waistcoat and powdered wig. The child itself, standing upright, moved its legs up and down as if operating the tricycle on which it perched. She wore a green dress made of real cloth, edged at the collar and waist with white braiding. Down the front of her dress were three buttons the size of dinner plates. On her feet were white ankle socks and leather sandals. She had bobbed black hair and a white, porcelain face with large brown eyes above a fixed, latex smile.

She was, despite her enormous size, extremely pretty.

Sid, who had never seen such an elaborate contraption before, was completely smitten. Mind you, since his most recent girlfriend had just dumped him for an impecunious rock star of dubious talent, a latex child that towered above his adoring eyes was quite a catch; or so he mused, as he followed her progress through the streets of London that particular spring morning.

Sid was a good-looking lad in his early thirties, with too many notches on his bed-head for comfort. His easy charm, Travolta-like looks and 'come-to-bed' eyes had entrapped many a young female - all of whom were resolutely dumped once consummation had been achieved; with Sid this usually took place on the first date. Some quickly saw through Sid's shallow charms and managed to dump him first; usually, however, it was the other way round. To fall, therefore, for a thirty-foot mechanical doll was not entirely unexpected, although the suddenness of his fixation was itself unusual. Those large brown eyes, severely bobbed hair and pale, sculptured face were irresistible. Sid, perhaps for the first time in his life, felt the tug of true love.

In strictly practical terms, it was a relationship doomed from the start.

Notwithstanding the vast disparity in their ages and the essential differences between human flesh and unyielding latex, the giant mechanical child was now moving down The Mall at an alarming speed, her operators pedalling like men possessed. Sid had to run just to keep abreast of his beloved little girl - well, not exactly 'little' but then love is blind, is it not?

The child's progress was slowed somewhat at the far end of the broad gravel path where it met a slight incline opposite Marlborough Road, causing the perspiring peddlers to falter. This allowed a breathless Sid time to catch up and position himself in front of the now stationary child.

Sometimes in life there are moments of such intensity, such emotional significance that they acquire the character and impact of some kind of life-changing force. Proust is full of such moments, as is James Joyce. Sid had never heard of either, let alone read them but he now knew exactly what they meant. This was one such moment as the gregarious, womanising Sid gazed lovingly into the plastic eyes of a thirty-foot doll on wheels. It was his epiphany.

Sid's life-style hitherto was that of a 1980's playboy - but without the means to fully support such a role. True, he had a passing resemblance to his hero John Travolta - an image he assiduously cultivated. His mates had once caught him walking up George Street, Romford dressed in tight jeans and T-shirt, carrying a can of paint in one hand. He was practicing 'The Walk'. Thereafter they teased him unmercifully, not because of the walk but because his pink i-Pod was stuffed with Bee Gee hits and other naff tracks of the period. In the end, Sid had the last laugh because girls loved the walk, the sharp suits from Ted Baker and his fantastic (albeit retro) dance style, again modelled on the Great JT. His looks might be a bit of a joke but his pulling power was legion (Sid's, that is - I can't speak for Travolta).

Sometimes the eyes play tricks and it was as Sid gazed adoringly into the plastic face of his new love that he now imagined that she was smiling directly at *him* and not at the crowd of onlookers who had also gathered beneath her towering figure. It was a smile of such purity, such utter devotion that Sid's heart literally missed a beat, his head swum and his legs went weak. Sid had never heard of Dante either but this moment of intense, albeit mute communication with his doll was not unlike Dante's first meeting with the beautiful, angelic Beatrice - only eight years and four months old at the time. When, therefore, the mechanical doll closed her right eye in what can only be described as a somewhat provocative wink, Sid virtually swooned with pleasure, fell to his knees on the pavement and wept for joy - probably for the first time in years.

Love is a strange phenomenon for it can sneak up on you when you least expect it. Sid, it must be said, had always avoided it - assiduously. Because most of the young girls he encountered were such easy prey, he had little overall respect for women in general. They were there for his pleasure or amusement and he could never, on principle, allow himself to be in their thrall - as often happens with those that are genuinely smitten. In short, love was a weakness to be avoided at all costs.

According to Sid's chauvinistic philosophy, girls were for pleasure - sexual pleasure. That was all there was to it.

Sid spent most weekends in Brighton. His friend Dave lived there in a small flat he called his 'Shag Pad' They had been friends since school and although Dave was a few years younger than Sid they had always got on well together. Dave was a cobbler by profession but at night he was a bouncer. He worked for an agency and would be moved from club to club as required. This gave Sid access to a wide range of venues, some as far away as Ramsgate or Margate. Where ever Dave was working that night, Sid was sure of easy access. While Dave lacked Sid's pulling power, bouncers could usually score most nights - especially if the young lady in question was desperate or drunk, or both.

When the clubs closed they would return to the 'Shag Pad', arm-in-arm with their respective partners for the night, and do the business - either on Dave's bed or on Sid's mattress in the spare room. Sometimes, if the young ladies were willing, they would swap partners in the night or if there was only one girl, share her - provided of course that she too was willing. Sid had had too many close shaves to risk being accused of statutory rape. He was, therefore, meticulous in such matters, only sleeping with entirely willing partners - even if they were occasionally under age.

The mechanical girl was now on the move once more, turning slowly left off The Mall and into St. James's Park itself. It was a delicate manoeuvre, requiring the two operators on her right hand side to pedal like men possessed while those on the left back-pedalled equally furiously. Slowly the giant doll on her tricycle moved off the gravel of The Mall and onto the bare grass of the park, some fifty feet or so from the road and close to the bandstand.

The elephant, having arrived there itself only ten minutes earlier, had already attracted a very large crowd. It was an impressive sight, what with its vast bulk and active trunk. Small boys kept running up to it, waving their arms and then scattering as it levelled its trunk and squirted buckets of water in their direction. This was accompanied by roars of laughter from the huge crowd, followed by spontaneous clapping - whereupon the liveried operators on the ornate platforms on the elephant's back and sides took a bow or two, again accompanied by appreciative clapping and the flash of countless digital cameras or mobile phones.

The mechanical girl took up position to the left of the elephant and soon attracted her own crowd of astonished onlookers - a curious mix of locals from the nearby government offices taking a short coffee break to see what all the fuss was about and foreign tourists, most of whom were armed with expensive video cameras. Sid pressed forward through the crowd until he was right at the front and able once more to gaze up at the adorable face of his beloved. She gazed back, with just the hint of an affectionate smile on her otherwise immobile face.

It was now late morning. The sun shone brightly and a light breeze stirred the trees in the royal park. London went about its business that day, largely unaware that a giant elephant and an exquisite, thirty-foot mechanical doll were in its midst - apart, that is, from some three hundred onlookers and a lovelorn Sid.
Sid was troubled. If this is love, he thought, then God help us all.

Even though he had deliberately avoided any lasting or deep-felt relationship, Sid had occasionally imagined at least that he was in love with some new 'bird'. This feeling, however, seldom lasted longer than it took to deftly remove her knickers and do the business. Flowers, boxes of chocolate and all that romantic stuff? Sure, he could do 'romantic' but so what? It was only a means to an end, after all. If that's what the soppy bitch wanted, so be it. The end result was always the same, however - a tasty shag and then a swift disengagement, shoving the poor girl out the back door if necessary, with or without the remains of her chocolates.

But this was different.

This mechanical doll, despite her size, was having such an effect on him that Sid had begun to doubt his sanity. True, she had expressed very little of her own feelings towards him as yet but they had only just met. It was early days and who could tell how things might develop?

It took ages for the crowds to finally disperse. Indeed, it was gone midnight before the park was empty and the curious had departed. Only a night guard remained and he spent most of his time in his caravan parked to one side of the two great mechanical figures. Sid, meanwhile, had found himself a deckchair in which he grabbed forty winks. However, as soon as all was quiet in the park and the night guard had done his rounds, he nervously approached the doll and stood at her feet, gazing longingly up at her adorable face. It was now two-thirty in the morning on a warm, spring night in London's St. James's Park - is that not the most perfect romantic setting?

'I don't know what to say but I think I love you,' Sid suddenly blurted out.
He spoke in a whisper that was probably loud enough to be heard as far away as Buckingham Palace - she was, after all, thirty feet tall.

'I know that this is crazy but I think you are wonderful. Could you possibly feel the same for me?'

The doll said nothing but gazed down at him in silence. Then, from the corner of one of her enormous brown eyes, there emerged a tear the size of a small bucket of water. It rolled down her extensive cheek and fell to the ground, splashing Sid's crocodile-skin winkle-pickers in the process.

'Please say you love me! Please, my darling. Please!'

Sid had never begged anything of a woman - ever. And yet here he was, kneeling at the foot of an enormous mechanical doll, pleading for his life. It was an entirely novel experience for his heart was full of such intense emotions that he could barely contain himself. The blood coursed through his body, his breath quickened and tears of love rolled down his own cheeks. He felt his knees tremble and when he looked at his hands he saw that they shook.

What then possessed him to climb up the doll is unclear. All that Sid could think was that he needed, desperately, to be close to his lovely girl, to whisper sweet nothings in her enormous ears and perhaps even kiss her delicate, latex lips.

To that end he at once hastily clambered up the scaffolding that enveloped her and from which hung her operators' four chairs. An elaborate system of ropes and wooden pulleys also hung from this aluminium frame, enabling her arms and legs to move and for the pedals of her tricycle to go up and down. Her wooden limbs were jointed and could, therefore, move when the whole apparatus was in motion. It was by using these ropes that Sid was able, eventually, to slide down and to hang, suspended, in front of her pale, exquisitely featured face.

It is difficult to describe adequately the feelings Sid felt at this precise moment; to be so close to his darling's lovely face with her brown, liquid eyes, delicate cheek bones and luscious mouth - now only inches from his own.

He tried to speak but the words stuck in his throat.

He longed to tell her of his innermost feelings, of his joy that they had met and of the regret that he also felt about the way he had treated other women - even if they were less adorable than she whom he now loved so passionately. He felt guilty at the callous way, hitherto, he had exploited women - especially young, innocent girls - for his own, selfish pleasure. He knew now that he had lamentably failed in his life to recognise and acknowledge the power of true love. Today, however, he was a changed man. Today, now that he had met *her*, he would honour women in ways worthy of their lovely, innate qualities. Above all, he loved her - passionately, inexplicably, excessively, and just as Dante had loved his Beatrice, Tristan his Isolde, Romeo his Juliet, Anthony his Cleopatra....

This list might have gone on indefinitely if Sid had not, at that precise moment, abandoned these unspoken thoughts and - man of action that he was - tried to kiss his beloved by leaning forward at an alarming angle whilst hanging by one arm on his length of rope. Unfortunately, he failed to make contact with his doll's enormous, albeit exquisite mouth and instead swung full circle at an alarming rate, missing her mouth completely. This sudden, circular movement caused him to lose his grip on the rope and abruptly fall to the ground, landing on the grass twenty feet below with a sickening thump.

What happened next was not only extraordinary but of a distinctly tragic nature; a tragedy witnessed, moreover, by the night guard who happened to emerge just then from his little caravan.

What he saw was Sid sprawled on the ground, clearly winded by his sudden fall. More importantly, the great doll that now towered above the prostrate lover was in the very process of breaking loose from her metal cage, ropes and pulleys and stepping off her enormous tricycle onto the grass. Once clear of the apparatus that had hitherto bound her, she made her first, faltering steps unaided towards an astonished Sid still lying on the ground. Her arms were extended in a gesture of such heartfelt concern for Sid that he too thought his heart might break there and then.

He was just about to get to his feet and run to greet her when the doll stumbled and fell, crushing him beneath her giant body. When the ambulance finally arrived it was too late for Sid was dead - even though there was a beatific smile on his handsome, lovelorn face.

7
Paradise Lost
(A cautionary tale)

Edward was not exactly fond of snails. While he thought them beautiful little creatures, perfectly formed and rather elegant with their finely mottled, pale grey skins and coloured shells, it would be wrong to say that he actually liked them.

However, his garden was full of them.

They were everywhere - lurking under flowerpots, behind the privet hedge and in every damp nook and cranny. One day he counted over a hundred and that was in a back garden that was barely big enough to contain a small bench, a dozen potted plants, a couple of mature bushes and a potting shed.

Edward lived alone in a small, Victorian house in a quiet part of Carlisle, off Myddleton Street. 29 Orfeur Street was the last terraced house in this little *cul-de-sac* with its pink sandstone pavements and cobbled road. Each house had a minute garden at the front, usually filled with potted geraniums and a small, walled garden at the back. A tall brick wall blocked the end of the street, beyond which were modern flats. This brick wall may have protected Edward and his neighbours from intruders but it did nothing to keep the snails at bay. They may be delicate little creatures but they ate Edward's plants just as fast as he added new ones to his garden. One evening he found the etiolated remains of a newly planted pot of parsley - *sans* leaves, *sans* everything. All that remained were the stems and they had been sucked of all their green chlorophyll - leaving only deathly white, flowerless stalks.

'That does it', said Edward. 'Enough is enough!'

Later that night, round about eleven o'clock, Edward collected over two-hundred-and- fifty snails in a plastic bucket and with a neighbour drove to Rickerby Park on the far side of the city. Here, by the light of a torch held by his friend Lesley, he gently emptied his bucket of snails onto the grass. This open land overlooked the banks of the River Eden. It was a beautiful spot and one that he was sure his snails would like. He and Lesley hastily left before a passing motorist perhaps noticed the suspicious activity of two individuals wearing day-glow rubber gloves and carrying a torch and an empty bucket.

The next night Edward repeated the process. This time, though, he discovered even more snails - big fat ones lurking behind the rose trellis at the bottom of his garden and under a large, upturned flowerpot he used for growing rhubarb. Thus some three hundred snails were gently deposited on fresh ground far away from his house and the temptations of his tiny garden. Once more he and Lesley, both wearing bright orange 'Marigold' gloves, hastily quit the scene of the crime like two guilty thieves, praying that no one had already reported them to the police.

For the next ten days Edward neglected his garden and collected no more snails. His first mistake!

Edward was, by profession, a freelance designer and a new tapestry project now fully occupied his thoughts. Each day he sat at his drawing board in the back bedroom he used as his studio, meticulously mixing his colours and blocking in each minute square of his needlepoint design drawn onto graph paper. It was highly skilled, painstaking work but the image that slowly emerged was very beautiful and would soon feature in an expensive catalogue and be turned - by numerous, nimble-fingered seamstresses - into elegant cushions or wall hangings.

Indeed, so busy was Edward with this project that he failed to notice the dozen or so snails that had gathered on the window of the same, first-floor room in which he laboured - snails, had he but realised it at the time, secretly watching his every move. Although their eyesight was poor, theses snails could certainly see, albeit dimly, their 'enemy' at work.

For days now they had been watching - and waiting.

It was late spring and the honeysuckle and Russian ivy in Edward's garden were now in full bloom. On warm evenings, after many hours in his studio, he would sit in his little garden and sip a glass of chilled Chardonnay, savouring the heady perfumes of his *Clematis Montana*, *Ceanthus* 'Blue Mound' and the potted *begonias* mixed with mauve flowered *pelargoniums* that he kept in a large tub by his sitting-room window.

Snails and other predatory creatures were far from his thoughts. His second major mistake!

It is not perhaps generally known that *Helix (Cyptoomphalus) aspersa* Müller (Gastropoda: Pulmonata: Helicidae) is a highly territorial creature with well-developed homing instincts. Thus it was that on the banks of the River Eden, some three miles from where Edward even then sipped his Chardonnay, an army of common garden snails was preparing for a perilous ascent - up the underside of the ancient stone bridge that crossed the river Eden north of the city. Snails can travel over fifty yards every hour but it had taken three days for the snails that Edward and his 'partner-in-crime' Lesley had dumped unceremoniously in a field to reach the river. Now they must cross it - by the only means at their disposal.

Meanwhile, Edward finished his wine, took a short tour of his garden, sniffed the newly opened *Paeonia suffruticosa* 'Situfukujin' and re-entered the house - carefully locking the door behind him before going to bed.
In the early hours of the following morning, five-hundred-and-fifty garden snails paused for breath - clamped to the damp stonework of the bridge on the far side of the River Eden.

Mission accomplished!

It had been a perilous journey, edging their way across the bridge. Some of the younger snails - lacking their elders' strength and experience - had plunged into the dark, swirling waters of the river far below them. Those that had survived must now wait for night before continuing their epic journey.

They were all exhausted by their heroic efforts but united in a common purpose - to regain the 'Lost Paradise' of Edward's small but luxuriant garden on the far side of the city; the garden from which they had been so cruelly expelled just a few days before.

Edward himself slept uneasily that night. He dreamt of snails and slugs crawling over his body, sucking at his eyelids or sliding into his open mouth. He woke up with a start, to find that the window of his bedroom was indeed covered with snails. He immediately went outside, still in his bare feet, placed a chair under the window, stood on it and with his broom gently brushed them away. Most survived this attack but some inevitably fell to the ground with a sickening crunch. When Edward picked them up he could see that their delicate, chestnut-coloured shells were smashed to smithereens.

He placed them all in a plastic bag - sad that he had, inadvertently, destroyed some of these harmless creatures.

Edward was a gentle soul. He had never unwittingly harmed anyone, least of all innocent gastropods. Less sensitive friends told him that he was silly and advised slug pellets or more drastic measures, such as 'stamping on the slimy buggers'. Edward refused, determined to respect the animals that inhabited his garden. This was not prompted by any religious belief. He was no Buddhist - merely someone who cared for others, including the common garden snail. However, he noticed that there were now more than ever in his garden. A further 'cull' was clearly necessary, followed by another trip to Rickerby Park. He rang Lesley and agreed a time for their third expedition north. He then filled another bucket with snails, covered it with cling film to prevent them escaping, and retired to his sitting room to await Lesley's arrival.

But Lesley did not arrive that evening. It had begun to rain heavily and it was decided to leave their expedition until the following evening. That did not happen either - for one reason or another - and the incarcerated snails in the covered bucket and plastic bag, together with those that had died, thus remained trapped for many more excruciating hours.

Edward's third serious mistake!

Throughout this period - unknown to Edward and the good citizens of Carlisle, including Lesley - a thick, slimy trail of snails was making its way past the Sands Leisure Centre, resolutely heading south towards Portland Square.

Leaving the bridge they had followed the river bank upstream until they found the golf course and could move swiftly through the short grass, pausing only for light refreshments *en route*. The statue of a heron at the back of the Sands had given some of the younger snails a momentary fright but they all reached the back of Trinity School via the playing fields relatively unscathed - apart from a brief attack by a fox rooting in dustbins behind the school's swimming pool.

Now began a particularly dangerous part of their journey in which they had to cross first Victoria Place (via Compton Street, adjacent to Carlisle College) before reaching the security of Chatsworth Square and the private park therein. Here they planned to rest during the day before making the highly dangerous journey to Portland Square itself - within striking distance of Edward's house and 'Snail Paradise'.

Meanwhile, Edward himself and his co-conspirator Lesley went about their separate business, totally unaware of the tragedy that was about to unfold.

After a day's recuperation in the private garden in the middle of Chatsworth Square, some five-hundred-and-eleven snails moved silently down Currie Street, using parked cars there as cover, and then across Chiswick Street and into a twisting back alley of flagstones and cobbles that eventually brought them to Spencer Street. Although Spencer Street was a particularly busy road, even at dead of night, they were able to use the privet hedge along the front of Devonshire House for cover and approach the dangerous crossing at Warwick Road and Brunswick unseen by even the few pedestrians still out and about.

Some did not survive the crossing that fateful night.

Although they crossed in small groups - to minimise accidents -

some thirty-seven tragically perished on Warwick Road alone, crushed by a speeding paramedic heading east. However, as dawn rose over an unsuspecting city, just over five hundred exhausted snails gathered together for safety beneath the beech trees in Portland Square. Here, amidst the rich leaf mould, tin cans and crisp packets they could snuggle together, mourn the loss of those that had died thus far and recharge their little batteries with a good day's sleep.

It was now Wednesday, 21st May.

One more day's travel and Edward's snails would be back home with their children and partners from whom they had been so cruelly separated. Even the hundred-and- thirty trapped in the bucket eventually ate their way through the cling-film under cover of night and hastily withdrew to their secret nooks and crannies in Edward's garden. Sadly, those trapped in the plastic bag slowly suffocated. Theirs had been a slow, excruciating death - despite the desperate efforts of friends and relatives to save them.

The following night (Thursday, 22nd May) some five-hundred intrepid snails left Portland Square, crossed Aglionby Street in the early hours of the morning and ascended the north face of No. 20.

It was an audacious tactic, equal in originality and daring to Hannibal's crossing of the Alps in 218 BC. Since time was now crucial, a direct ascent up the front of this large Victorian house, a trip across the tiles (dangerously exposed to predatory gulls), a perilous descent down the other side and off over the back fence was deemed appropriate to their needs. Indeed, it would shorten their journey by some five hundred yards.

The next morning, when the occupants of 20 Aglionby Street sat down for coffee in their garden, they were horrified to see that their pride *Hosta lancifolia* had been completely shredded - the victim, had they but known it, of hundreds of peckish snails. Had they looked even more closely they might also have seen a slimy trail that ascended their back fence, skirted along the top of the old brick wall at the side of the house behind them and on into Orfeur Street itself - and the 'Paradise Regained' of Edward's little garden.

That weekend Edward had visited friends in Newcastle and was therefore unaware of the triumphant arrival on the morning of Saturday, 23rd May at his house of a small army of exhausted snails, each of whom scaled his garden wall to be reunited in an orgy of slime with their friends and relatives. It was a glorious homecoming, celebrated in an ecstasy of viscous couplings and glutinous reconciliations, culminating in the fervent fertilization of over seven thousand tiny eggs.

Edward returned from Newcastle on Sunday evening, took a stroll round his garden and retired to bed - forgetting to close his kitchen window.

This was his fourth mistake and one that would prove fatal.

When the police broke in three days later after friends and neighbours had raised the alarm, they found Edward stretched out on his bed, naked. He was deathly white, as if the colour had been completely sucked from his body.

There were no signs of the thousands of snails that had entered his house that night (Sunday, 24th May - National Escargot Day) and who had then made their silent way up his stairs and into his bedroom. Deep in sleep - the larger part of a fine bottle of Chardonnay having been consumed earlier that evening - Edward had probably felt nothing as over two thousand snails completely covered him in their glutinous embrace and sucked him dry with their ribbon-like tongues.

With their deadly mission accomplished and revenge finally exacted, they returned to their garden as silently as they had left it.

8
The Thief of Baghdad

On a remote island in the Venetian lagoon, three men gathered driftwood at the water's edge before lighting a fire round which they then squatted. It was a dark, February night, threatening snow. The still waters of the lagoon shone inky black as the moon emerged - then vanished as quickly and as mysteriously as it had appeared.

The lunatic asylum that once dominated San Clemente was now a pile of ancient rubble but one stone tower remained and it was from here that a fourth man, wrapped in a ragged blanket, first saw the approaching boat. It appeared like a ghost out of the mist, its prow scraping fragments of rounded brick as it ran aground. A young man, as dark as the night itself, leapt ashore to be greeted warmly by the others. His name was Ibrahim but to the Venetian police he would soon become known as the 'Thief of Baghdad'.

A wild dog at the far end of the island, disturbed by these visitors to an otherwise uninhabited island, suddenly began to howl. The men, startled, rapidly extinguished their fire then disappeared into the darkness.

Jan Wynman, seated at his table in the Piazza San Marco, first warmed his hands on his glass of Russian tea, took a sip, placed his glass carefully back on the white tablecloth then picked up his copy of 'L'Arena'.

'A vandal with a hammer and chisel and an obsession with smashing stone hands has galvanised Venice into frightened awareness of the vulnerability of its priceless heritage.'

Jan removed his glasses, polished them briefly with the corner of his napkin, and returned to his newspaper.

'The attacker has now struck three times since being spotted at 10.30 on Saturday morning in St. Mark's Square and swinging his hammer at one of the intricately worked capitols on the face of the cathedral.'

Jan took another sip of tea. The wintry sun that had covered St. Mark's Square was now dipping fast behind the Campanile, causing a dark shadow to spread across the almost deserted square. Jan drained the remains of his lukewarm tea and resumed his reading.

'The Piazza San Marco was still crowded with visitors but it took an art-loving vendor with a push-cart to raise the alarm and give chase, unsuccessfully.'

A waiter appeared, removed Jan's empty glass, and deftly substituted his soiled ashtray with one that was pristine clean. He then scuttled back to the warmth of Florian's sumptuous interior. It was now six-twenty. The small crowd that had gathered near the entrance to the Basilica San Marco was still watching a policeman, balanced precariously on a ladder, taking photographs of the vandalised capitol.

The hands of the figure of Moses had been smashed, as had the mosaic tablets of the laws once held by them.

Jan lit another cigarette and resumed his reading.

'On the Giudecca, carvings of St. Martin and St. Francis outside the Church of the Most Holy Redeemer were also damaged. The fingers on three of the four hands were amputated.'

Jan folded his paper, threw a few coins onto the table and left, flicking his cigarette into a puddle. He quit the square via the Piazzetta and headed towards the Grand Canal. By now it was almost dark and a sharp wind off the lagoon rippled the black water. Jan shivered, turned up the collar of his camel-hair coat and leant into the wind. He took the first available *motoscafo* and disembarked, ten minutes later, at the Accademia Bridge.

Jan was Dutch architect, now thirty-two. Although educated in Utrecht, his Catholic family had lived in Italy since he was a child; he therefore both knew and loved the country well. Although he had first practised architecture in Antwerp he had always preferred the sunlight of Italy to the cold wind and rain of his native land and in 1998 had therefore moved his practice to Milan, with offices also in Rome and Trieste. The following year he bought a large Venetian apartment on the Fondamenta Bragadin, overlooking Rio di San Vio.

This particular apartment had once belonged to the Englishman who first introduced Guinness (served ice cold) to an unsuspecting Venetian clientele. He had become very rich in the process and had modernised his luxury, third-floor apartment with great taste. Now it was Jan's 'bolt hole' from the pressures of work. However, being something of a 'workaholic', he usually ended up combining work with pleasure. Jan loved the apartment's clean, functional lines and contemporary fixtures and fittings. His only addition to its décor was five signed photographs by Robert Mapplethorpe in the lounge; a large oil painting by Ysbrandt van Weingaarden in the dining room and some pornographic prints that had once belonged to Rudolf Nureyev. These he had hung in his bedroom.

Jan poured himself a fine malt whisky and flicked on the television. The activities of the vandal had now reached the national television screens.

'It was discovered yesterday that the sculpture of St. Peter outside the Church of San Pietro di Castello, on the island of the same name, has been disfigured.'
At this point the news cut away from the female newsreader to a close-up of the damaged figure, the freshly exposed stone clearly visible.

'This sculpture depicts St. Peter receiving the key from the Holy Infant cradled in the arms of the Virgin Mary.'

The newsreader appeared once more.

'Police believe the same person is responsible for all three incidents. They are the first such acts of vandalism in living memory in Venice, but other parts of Italy have grown wearily familiar with lunatics with hammers.'

Jan flicked off the television and retreated to his spacious studio at the back of the apartment - where he worked until three in the morning. That night he dreamed that someone with an axe hacked off both his hands.

Dawn spread its golden light across the lagoon, sucking up the sea mist in vertical spirals and gilding the choppy waves. Stumpy, wooden piles (*bricole*) defined the channels, creating elegant parabolas that criss-crossed the expanse of dark green water as far as the eye could see.

Because of its shifting mud flats and swirling channels, the Venetian lagoon is a dangerous place at the best of times but in winter it can be very treacherous indeed. However, Jan knew these waters well and steered his motorboat towards the island of Torcello, deftly avoiding the numerous sand banks that lay before him. With the wind on his face and the taste of salt in the air, he found this short journey across the lagoon exhilarating.

Jan had known Torcello since he was a child. Most Sundays he had attended mass there with his devout parents and had come to love the island's Byzantine cathedral. Once this small island had had a population of some twenty thousand but now a mere sixty lived there. Having moored his boat near the vaporetto landing-stage, Jan strolled along the canal bank towards the cathedral. He could feel the morning sun on his back. Birds sang and memories of his beloved parents filled his heart. They were still alive but, due to the pressures of his busy practice, he seldom saw them now. It was time, he resolved there and then, to pay them a visit in Vicenza - before they were gone for ever.

Jan entered the ancient cathedral, dipped his fingers in holy water near the main entrance and genuflected, his eyes naturally drawn to the 13th Century Madonna and Child high above the altar in the apse - one of the loveliest mosaics in Italy. He sat on a wooden chair at the back, said a brief prayer for his elderly parents then leant back to soak up the atmosphere of this hauntingly beautiful place. It was too early for the usual influx of tourists, even in February, so Jan had the basilica to himself - or so it seemed.

It was then that he noticed a young man kneeling by the rood screen. He was gazing intently at the *Iconostasis* - exquisite Byzantine marble panels at the base of the screen. Even from

where he sat Jan could see that the boy was slim, very handsome and with large brown eyes. His black hair was cut very short but the curve of his skull and the exposed nape of his neck sent shivers of desire down Jan's spine. As he watched, the boy reached out with his left hand and gently stroked the two peacocks drinking from the fountain of life. Jan stared, fascinated by the boy's tentative movements - like a blind man exploring some beautiful vase or sculpture. Suddenly, the boy looked up, saw Jan staring at him, turned on his heels and, quickly crossing the nave, left the cathedral by a side door. By the time Jan reached the grass courtyard by the main entrance the boy had disappeared.
Two days later Venice was buzzing with news of another act of vandalism, this time within the Doge's Palace.

It seems that a night watchman, wandering the corridors of the palace, stumbled on a young man in the act of cutting off the right hand of one of the two great statues on the *Scala dei Giganti*. The vandalised figure was that of Sansovino's 'Neptune'. By the time the guard raised the alarm and reached the central courtyard the boy had escaped. Several arrests were made later of likely candidates but no one believed that this was the act of some lunatic vagrant. To get into the palace was not difficult - security was lax - but this act of vandalism was itself well planned, for the vandal had not only remained hidden after closing time but had used a cordless, circular-saw to sever Neptune's right hand at the wrist. This latest act of vandalism had taken place within yards of the offices of the Ministry of Culture and Architectural Heritage, thereby adding insult to injury.

That evening Jan dined with a friend at his favourite Venetian restaurant - 'Locanda Montin'- near the Zattere. Here the walls were covered in original paintings, including a small canvas by Picasso, an exquisite still life by Matisse and many others of more dubious provenance. Moreover, the waiters all wore tartan waistcoats - something Jan had always found faintly ludicrous.

Conversation over supper was largely about the recent attack on the great statute of Neptune. Gabriella Rogliani - herself a former curator at the Uffizi Gallery in Florence - was alarmed. Although such attacks were new to Venice, Florence had already suffered similar acts of artistic vandalism.

'In 1991,' she recalled, 'a deranged artist called Piero Cannata attacked   Michelangelo's 'David'. He broke one of his toes.'

'Whose? David's or one of his own?'

'It's not a joking matter, Jan. This lunatic is serious. Who next? Indeed, what
 statue is safe now?'

'Venus de Milo?' he volunteered.
Jan chuckled at his somewhat lame joke and tucked into his fegato alla Veneziana. Gabriella remained unconvinced and scowled at him. She was a tall, slim Florentine academic with grey eyes and a long pony tale. Jan was inordinately fond of her but, like many Fine Art scholars, she was sometimes short on humour.

'My dear Gabriella,' Jan added, sensing her frown, 'You are far too serious. Art
 should not last for ever. One way or another it must change. All this lunatic is doing is accelerating that process. Besides, I think I have seen him.'

'You've *seen* him? When?'

'Yesterday, on Torcello. He was in the basilica, admiring the *Iconostasis.*'

'But how do you know that it was him?'

'Instinct. He was, moreover, very good looking!'

At that point a tartan waiter poured them both another glass of fine Bardolino and the conversation immediately switched to their respective lovers.

When Jan got home that night, slightly the worse for wear, he rang his house in Milan. Giovanni was not there. This was the second, consecutive night that he had failed to answer Jan's call. While they both gave each other certain freedom, theirs was a well-established relationship so that Giovanni's lack of communication with his lover of some seven years was always worrying. That night Jan dreamed not of Giovanni but of the young Arab boy.

Two days later it was time to leave Venice. Jan packed his suitcase and gathered together his architectural drawings - the product of many hours of work during his short stay in Venice. What had begun as a vacation had ended in a flurry of creativity but tomorrow he must leave for Trieste for a meeting with his agent and to check a new office-block that was nearing completion.

That evening - likely to be his last in Venice for some months - he decided to treat himself to a drink at Harry's Bar, followed by a concert at the 'Fenice' then supper with Gabriella at a nearby restaurant. None of this happened for on his way to the Calle Vallaresso he rounded a corner and nearly bumped into the dark-skinned boy. For a moment they stared at each other, mutually transfixed - then the boy darted off, disappearing into the shadows of a nearby *calle*. He was carrying under his arm a small object, wrapped in newspaper.

Jan instinctively took chase - just in time to see the boy disappear round another corner, clearly now aware that he was being followed.

Jan was not sure whether it was lust or curiosity that now prompted him to follow this strange young man yet he was determined to confront him, whatever the outcome. Who knows, perhaps he *was* the celebrated vandal whose acts of violence were now the talk of Venice? Either way, Jan felt compelled to follow but what would he do if he caught up with him? What he *did* know was that he found this mysterious boy immensely attractive - with his large brown eyes, slim, muscular body and furtive manner.

Although Jan was not, by nature, sexually promiscuous, he had occasionally been drawn to younger men or boys - particularly those at the 'rough' end of the trade. After such lapses he had always been consumed with Catholic guilt - much to Giovanni's amusement. Perhaps this strange encounter with the young Arab was to be yet another 'lapse' but then some dark premonition told him somehow that this was to be a very different kind of encounter and one that would change him for ever. It was with these troubled thoughts racing through his head that he turned the corner and continued his pursuit of the dark-skinned boy.

It was carnival time and although still only about seven in the evening on a frosty February night, masked revellers were already making their way towards the boats that would take them to Murano for the evening's festivities. The men mostly wore white Commedia del'Arte masks and long, black cloaks. The women, however, were dressed very extravagantly - beautiful gold masks, ornate hats, long sweeping gowns covered in silver braid and highly embroidered shawls, often covered in fine lace and encrusted with costume jewellery.

Jan did not like carnivals. His life was neat, well-ordered and planned - by and large. These bacchanalian events were far too anarchic for his taste so it was with some unease that he sidestepped two revellers in full costume - masks, feathers and long red gowns - that momentarily blocked his way. A third figure, with the mask of a skull and a funereal cloak and cape, suddenly appeared round another corner. Jan quickly stepped into a doorway and allowed the ghostly figure to sweep past him, instinctively crossing himself in the process. By the time he reached the end of this twisting *calle* the boy had completely vanished.

Often Venice can surprise even those who, like Jan, had many times experienced its peculiar magic.

As he crossed the Accademia Bridge the moon appeared and bathed everything in its deathly light. Myriad stars shone in an ebony-black sky. Revellers strolled across the bridge dressed in eighteenth-century costumes - as if in a slow-motion dream. There was laughter and music and, on the far side of the city, fireworks began to burst into the night sky. People stopped, stared and pointed at the illuminated horizon. Through the mouth-holes of their grotesque masks emerged the ghostly, clouded breath of each frozen reveller.

Jan quickly left the bridge and headed for the Campo Santo Stefano. This large square was dotted with groups of revellers huddled together - as if trying to gain warmth from each other. Children ran about excitedly, hurling handfuls of flour at unwary pedestrians. Jan carefully skirted these little monsters and left the square via Calle dello Spezier, heading for Campo san Mauritzio. He had, unconsciously, abandoned his chase. Indeed, all thoughts of the boy had mysteriously vanished and all he could think now was that he was late for the concert at the Fenice that he had booked earlier that day. He entered the square and began to run, feeling the cold night air on his face and exposed hands. He had forgotten his gloves.

Suddenly, some instinct or momentary premonition told him to stop and look up.

There, hanging from the underside of the balcony of a large house on his side of the square was the dark-skinned boy who, only minutes earlier, he had been chasing. The balcony itself was on the floor above the *piano nobile* and consisted of a stone platform and ornate balustrade, supported by two marble statues. The boy was actually clinging to the underside of the balcony, his legs hanging free some sixty feet above the pavement. Jan at once ran to the house, just in time to see a metal saw fall to the pavement, landing only inches from where he now stood.

It was clear that the boy was in some difficulty for he clung to the underside of the balcony by one hand while trying desperately to clamber back up. Even from where he stood Jan could see that the right hand of one of the monumental statues supporting the balcony had been severely vandalised in an attempt to remove it completely. It was then that Jan also noticed that the pavement beneath his feet was scattered with broken masonry, including three stone fingers.

After several frantic attempts to gain entry to the house, Jan found a side door that was unlocked, promptly entered the building and ran up three flights of stairs as fast as he could - to discover, on the top landing, a wooden ladder leading to a skylight in the roof. Perhaps this was the way the boy himself had gained access to the balcony. Either way, it provide Jan with the access he urgently needed.

When he emerged onto the roof itself the cold air struck him like a sharp blow to the face. As an architect he was used to heights and was able therefore to make his way down the tiles towards the front of the building. Peering over the gutter he could see the boy, visibly tiring as he tried to swing his legs back onto the parapet. Jan slipped over the edge of the roof and dropped lightly onto the balcony, some six feet below. He was now within eighteen inches of the young man.

'Give me your hand. I can help you.'

With his free hand the boy instinctively reached up towards Jan's outstretched arm. Far below a small crowd had gathered, watching intently.

'Come on! You can do it.'

Jan grabbed the boy's hand, took the strain and began to pull him slowly towards the balcony's edge and safety. For a moment he hung there, starring into his rescuer's eyes with a look that inexplicably sent shivers down Jan's spine.

Suddenly the young Arab plunged to the ground.

Jan stared in utter astonishment as the crowd quickly gathered round the body, now sprawled obscenely on the pavement far below. Blood began to ooze from his head onto the stone flags. A policeman, scrambling over the tiles towards Jan, also stopped in his tracks, astonished by this sudden turn of events.

Jan slumped to the ground, clasped his knees with both arms and leant back against the parapet. He was in deep shock, with the young man's dying screams still ringing in his ears.

The policeman dropped down onto the balcony beside him, bent down and touched Jan gently on the shoulder.

'You alright, sir?'

Jan said nothing but began to shake uncontrollably.

'You did all you could sir, I'm sure.'

Jan closed his eyes, trying to shut out the vision of the boy's crumpled body lying on the pavement sixty feet below them.

'It seems he was an illegal immigrant,' added the policeman. 'They come in through the lagoon, at night. We caught three of them only a week ago but this one escaped. We know from the Iraqi police that he had stolen a woman's handbag some months ago. She was from the Italian embassy in Baghdad. She reported him to the local authorities who punished him in the usual way. Barbaric, I call it. His real name was Ibrahim but we called him the 'Thief of Baghdad'. Poor little bugger! He was only just sixteen.'

It was only then that Jan realised that he was still clutching the boy's artificial right hand.

9
Gerald's Greek holiday

According to the police, Gerald was a ticking bomb just waiting to explode. Of course Gerald saw it otherwise. He had never done anything wrong. True, he had been cautioned a number of times but that is all. 'Innocent until proven guilty'. Is that not what they say?

Every Saturday morning Gerald took the bus from Workington into Carlisle for a bit of shopping. After a cup of tea and an egg barmcake in the covered market, he would take the escalator up to the apartment store above the market where he would quietly examine the racks of children's underwear.

He was a tall, thin, balding man in his late fifties and a familiar figure in Carlisle. But what could you do? He did no harm and never spoke to anyone and generally minded his own business. After a while the staff stopped staring nervously and simply ignored him. All, that is, except the security man at the door - a muscular individual with a shaven head.

For Gerald, these stolen moments amongst the racks of diminutive knickers were excruciatingly pleasurable. He examined each garment in turn, preferring to handle those of pure cotton rather than of mixed, modern fibres, The simpler the better, he thought. Those with frills and lacy bits were wholly inappropriate, especially for little girls brought up properly. His mother, long since dead, had been very strict in such matters. His sisters only wore the purest cotton, even if mother had to scrimp and save to buy them. They were a poor, working-class family from Wigton but highly respectable - or so his mother always insisted.

After a while Gerald would leave the store and walk up to Tesco's where he bought his provisions for the week. He would then catch the bus back to Workington. This was how he spent his Saturdays. On Sundays he would sleep in, then get up and watch telly all day or surf the net. He knew it was wrong to look at child pornography but that was his nature. If it was God's intention that he should be that way inclined, so be it. There was nothing he could do about it anyway. 'Say-lavee', as his mother always said.

Gerald worked for the local council in Workington. It was a boring job, processing parking tickets, but the pay was steady. He was not particularly popular at work but at least they left him alone. Elsewhere he had been bullied and abused - but for what? For being Gerald? Hardly a crime, surely? His neighbours were less sanguine. Some had tried to get him moved to another council flat but since he had done nothing wrong he stayed put. Occasionally some lout would put a brick through his front window or something worse through his letter box but he kept his dignity and battled on, keeping himself to himself.

He had been planning his holiday now for two years, scrimping and saving to pay for it. He had never been abroad before - other than to the Isle of Man once, with his mother, on his sixteenth birthday.

Greece seemed to him like an exotic country on the far side of the moon. He spent hours pouring over brochures, examining each coloured photograph carefully and planning his holiday down to the smallest detail. His case was packed two weeks before the actual departure date, so excited was he at the prospect of this first real holiday.

At last the great day arrived!

He took the coach from Carlisle to Manchester and arrived five hours before he was due to check in. He was the first in the queue. At customs they took their time examining his new passport, the man behind the desk giving him that fixed, penetrating stare they do. Gerald felt very uncomfortable and for one dreadful moment thought that they were about to arrest him but then the man waved him through with an abrupt flick of his hand.

The flight to Athens - his first experience on an aeroplane, even at the age of fifty-seven - was exhilarating. Although he talked to no one throughout the journey he enjoyed every minute of the long flight, eating both meals with all the fastidious pleasure of an experienced, much-travelled gourmet. He was used to take-away meals so he was able to unwrap the tin foil packages with his long, thin fingers without burning himself. His treat was a large gin-and-tonic which he managed to make last for at least an hour.

The coach trip from Athens to the Pelion peninsular was less enjoyable. It took nearly four hours. Only when they reached the mountains and the winding coastal road did he perk up. The views from the bus of the Panaglistic Gulf were stunning. By now it was early evening. The glint of sunlight on the water, the silver grey outline of the bay shaped like a scimitar, and the dozens of tiny sail boats dotted about made his heart skip a beat or two.

The little pension in Horto was not quite like the photographs in his brochure but at least it was reasonably clean. His mother had always been fastidious in matters of personal hygiene so Gerald felt obliged to polish the sink and lavatory bowl himself, once he had unpacked. His few clothes, hung neatly in the cupboard, smelled of mothballs.

From the window of his tiny bedroom he could see the harbour. The stony beach was covered in litter but a line of plane trees hung with coloured lights gave the front a jaunty, seaside look. It was a good choice for a holiday, not least because so far the coastal and mountain villages of Pelion were unspoilt. There were a few new villas but as yet no ugly hotels catering for coach trippers and their like. Gerald closed the curtains, undressed, folded his clothes neatly on a chair, climbed into his woollen pyjamas and got into bed. He immediately fell asleep. It had been a long day.

Horto had been spared the great earthquake of 1953 so that it still contained a number of handsome, 19th Century houses. In between there were modern buildings, catering for the largely Greek or German families who came to Horto for their annual holiday. On the harbour itself there were several small restaurants, and a shabby bar or two but no shops. At the back of the village, near the main road, Gerald found a mini-mart and purchased a tin of Nescafe, a jar of local honey and a pot of Greek yoghurt. He was too shy as yet to try out the few phrases of Greek he had taught himself back home in Workington. Anyway, the shopkeeper spoke perfect English.

After breakfast in his room Gerald went for a stroll along the seafront. It was a gorgeous day, the sun already quite hot. He had plastered his face and legs with suntan lotion so there was little chance of getting burnt on this, his first proper day abroad. He felt a bit odd in his aertex shirt and baggy shorts but 'When in Rome', as his mother used to say.

He took lunch at a small tavern close to the jetty. There were a number of solid wooden tables and chairs, set in rows on the beach itself. Plastic tablecloths with lurid flower patterns added colour to an otherwise drab little restaurant. However, the large canopy of plane trees afforded ample shade from the noonday sun. Tiny, emaciated sparrows cavorted at his feet in dust bowls of their own making, surrounded by fag ends and used bottle tops. The occasional gull swooped, savaging on the distant shore line.

Gerald ordered meat balls and chips. He had never drunk wine so instead he chose a German beer. The boy who served him was called Toto. He was seventeen, as brown as a berry and with shiny white teeth. Gerald ate his meatballs and chips, drank his ice-cold German beer and luxuriated in the knowledge that he was now actually in Greece, on holiday and with a whole week still to go.

By now the sun had turned the bay a golden yellow. On the concrete jetty a large family had gathered - parents, aunts and uncles and even Grandma. The children kept jumping in and out of the water. They were a noisy bunch, laughing and shouting. Very boisterous, or so Gerald thought. From where he sat - sipping his beer and trying to make it last - they took on the appearance of strange, magical shapes silhouetted against the fierce, afternoon sun. They moved as if in a dream, almost in slow motion, like languid moths trapped against the glass of a dusty, sun-drenched window.

She appeared out of nowhere - a slim, brown figure in a pink gingham bikini, playing at the water's edge. She had the elfin looks of Audrey Hepburn, or so Gerald thought. Her body was that of an eight-year-old and yet she possessed pert little breasts that amply filled her minute bikini top. She moved more like a boy than a little girl, squatting at the water's edge, playing in the mud or splashing her companion. He was only slightly older but he had none of the grace and charm of this beautiful Greek child. He was called Minos but he never once called her by name so Gerald never found out what she was called.

Later that day, in a narrow alleyway behind the car-park adjacent to the fetid canal, Gerald was seen offering this enchanting child an ice cream.

He was promptly arrested, taken to the nearest police station at Argostellini and then transferred two days later to a squalid cell in a prison on the outskirts of Athens - to await trial. He languished in this prison for seven weeks. Conditions were indescribable and he became very depressed, crying himself to sleep most nights. When his deranged cell- mate tried to rape him he was put into solitary confinement.

Later, much later, they moved him to another prison on a remote Greek island, far from the city. Deportation was ruled out by the local Magistrate and Gerald has yet to meet his defence lawyer or even someone from the British Consulate. As weeks stretched into months he became more and more depressed and twice tried to hang himself in his cell, failing miserably each time.

No date has yet been set for his trial.

Such are the vagaries of love. Thus ended Gerald's Greek holiday. As the song says: 'Too much love will kill you in the end'.

10
Antonio's Revenge

It is said that inside every fat man there is a thin one struggling to get out. Antonio did not believe that, despite his grotesque size - until one morning his fat body split apart, revealing a tall, thin naked figure surrounded by buckets of blubber, mucus and blood.

Antonio had always been fat. He was sixteen pounds when his mother thrust him forth into a world of thin men and women. She nearly died in the process. Despite the surgeon's knife and some eleven hours of shoving and pushing, Antonio at first refused to come out - as if somehow he knew what cruel fate awaited him. When eventually he emerged, two midwives had to carry him to the scales. His poor mother fainted when she saw him but perhaps that was really to do with the supreme effort taken to effect his monstrous birth.

Antonio was born hungry. At the first available opportunity he grabbed his mother's breasts and sucked both dry. The poor woman had to endure this orgy of greed five or six times a day for at least three years, by which time Antonio was the size of a baby elephant - or so their neighbours thought.

Antonio prospered, growing fatter by the day. The tree, planted to celebrate his birth, grew tall and thin - as if to mock its celebrant's alarming size. His father - for he was an odd man in many ways - had buried his son's placenta when he planted the tree. Each year this flowering cherry sprouted blood-red blossom, although its branches remained resolutely thin.

School for Antonio was a nightmare. Children can be cruel and a fat child is a target not to be ignored. Throughout his school days Antonio was bullied and derided, reducing him to tears each night as he rolled onto his (reinforced) bed in the seaside town of Porto Maurizio on the Italian Riviera. He was a slow child, poor at his studies and therefore unable to outdo his tormentors academically. His mental state was not helped by his teachers who, in their own way, were as cruel as the children they taught. His geography teacher, in particular, was profoundly insensitive and regularly called Antonio a 'stupid tub of lard'. Although this was essentially true, Antonio had feelings like anyone else. Indeed, the hurt *he* felt within his enormous body was, if anything, more acute than that felt by any ordinary Italian adolescent.

Each day, as he suffered their taunts and jibes, he grew bitter and resentful - until he was a vast balloon of obese anger ready to burst.

Most adolescents find love in one form or another. Antonio was no exception. He actually fancied a number of girls but they would rather be dead than be seen with him. He knew this because they told him - repeatedly. There was always masturbation. Like any boy of his age, he indulged his sexual fantasies and obtained a measure of physical relief this way but it was no substitute for the real thing. At the age of fifteen he was, therefore, still a virgin - an extraordinarily fat virgin, weighing nearly twenty-two stones.

He left school with few qualifications but obtained a job as a clerk in an insurance office in Alassio, just up the coast from Porto Maurizio. It was mostly menial work, such as photocopying and filing. He coped with this reasonably well but throughout his working day had to endure the taunts of even senior management. Deep down, his fellow office-workers felt embarrassed by his cumbersome presence in their midst. Few befriended him or even tried to understand his feelings. He went home each evening, seething with resentment.

Antonio continued to live in the family home in Porto Maurizio, reluctantly commuting each day to Alassio by train.

Occasionally, at weekends, he ventured down onto the beach. He was too fat to get into the little wooden changing rooms that lined the promenade so he changed at home, then disrobed at the water's edge where he sat, like a marooned whale, gazing out to sea. Of course people stared but once he had ventured into the water he became oblivious to their taunts. Buoyed up by the salty water, even his enormous bulk floated serenely. He luxuriated in this temporary state of weightlessness, wallowing in the shallows like a basking shark.

On such occasions - if only for half an hour or so in his fat, miserable life - he became truly happy.

Antonio led a very lonely life, not least because his loving and indulgent mother had died only seven years after his birth - worn out, probably, with the supreme effort required to constantly nurture her gargantuan child. His father had done his best but he was a shallow, somewhat self-absorbed individual with little time for a boy whom he secretly considered a freak. He was tall and thin - something that made Antonio even more conscious of his extreme corpulence. Antonio's father withdrew into his study (he was Professor of Economics at the university in Genoa) and effectively 'looked the other way' for years until he too died. Antonio was nineteen when he buried him. It was, to be honest, a relief to both parties - father and son alike.

The next two years were something of a nightmare.

Antonio now weighed a staggering twenty-seven stones. Even the most basic movement was almost impossible for him so that he had to quit the job in Alassio and live as best he could at home in Porto Maurizio. He spent a large part of the day propped up in bed watching television - and eating junk food or sumptuous Ligurian pasta dishes. His favourite was gnocchi covered in a rich, green pesto - a speciality of the region. He could consume five bowls of this stuff each day; excellent food in itself but only in moderation.

Moderation was *not* a term with which Antonio was familiar.

On his twenty-first birthday he inherited sufficient money from his parsimonious father to afford someone to look after him fulltime. Angelica, his tireless nurse, was a generous, working-class soul who did much to alleviate his suffering. She was about fifty-five but very sprightly and came from the medieval mountain village of Apricale.

She was as brown as a walnut and twice as tough but with a mouth on her that was not celebrated for its tact. However, Angelica adored her portly patron and attended to most of his needs, refusing only to wipe his bottom. This he had to do himself, with considerable difficulty I might add.

Despite Angelica's best efforts, Antonio's mental state was worsening. He now had such low self-esteem that he often felt suicidal - but without the courage to activate such a dramatic 'solution'. Each day that passed he slid, inexorably, into an ever deeper 'slough of despond'. He was now nearly thirty-two stones - a gargantuan heap of a man and with a face so fat that he could barely see. Even the ever-optimistic Angelica began to despair, fearful for his future - and said so, much to his dismay. Indeed, he was so upset that he sacked her on the spot. She packed her bags and left that same day - in floods of tears whilst muttering, simultaneously, Ligurian oaths of a darkly litigious nature.

With Angelica gone he was now alone - fat and increasingly helpless. His future looked very bleak.

The day of his rebirth dawned, unexpectedly, one September morning. Mists still covered the mountains above Imperia but already dozens of house-martins were flying hither and thither, chasing air-born insects. From his bedroom window Antonio could see them. He had always enjoyed their swoops and dives, their effortless flight. If only he could move with such grace, such sublime freedom - would that not be something special, something unique? There were tears in his piggy eyes as he pondered this, longing to escape the glutinous, obese prison that his enormous body had become.

Inside, there really was a thin man now trying to escape but even Antonio, in his wildest dreams, knew that that was mere fantasy, trapped as he was in a veritable 'tub of lard'.

What happened next began quietly enough - with the merest sensation at the back of his enormous neck, followed by a brief but intense stab of pain. The split that had opened up at the base of Antonio's skull now spread up the back of his head, across the top and down his forehead. Blood began to trickle down his face, momentarily blinding him. Then, with a suddenness that was especially alarming, the split abruptly ran the length of his face, dividing his mouth in two and disappearing under his chin. The flesh that had once covered his head next rolled off his skull and fell, like flaps of wet chamois leather, onto his naked shoulders.

He knew of course that something extraordinary, something unique was happening to him but he did not panic. Instead, he struggled to his feet, heaving his enormous bulk into an upright position. It was at this point - as he stood, swaying and breathless at the foot of his bed - that the split, now at his throat, suddenly ran the length of his chest, opening up a bloody fissure and exposing the raw carcass within. Antonio stared down in horror as his chest cavity split apart, then travelled the length of his gigantic stomach. At the same time the flesh slipped from his shoulders like an abandoned overcoat and hung around his waist like a pile of offal stripped from the stomach cavity of a slaughtered pig.

Antonio screamed, not with the pain but in horror and shock. His screams reverberated round the bedroom and spread throughout the house but no one heard them for he was alone.

This was not, however, a dream!

Even as he stood there, transfixed with fear and disgust, the flesh fell in folds from his hips and thighs, then knees and calves until it lay in obscene heaps at his feet on the wet tiles of his bedroom floor. Piles of fat and skin, smeared with blood and mucus, now stretched in all directions - like the remains of a butchered whale. Some of the liquid glycerol and fatty acids had even begun to ooze their way onto his landing and down the stairs.

It was at this point that Antonio - or what was left of him - fainted, falling to the blood-stained tiles where he lay, unconscious, for several hours.

When he awoke it was night. Light from the street lamp by his bedroom window revealed the carnage, still lying in horrendous globules of semi-liquid fat and shreds of flesh at the foot of his bed. He gingerly stepped over the mess and moved to the landing where he was at least able to shut the door of his bedroom, thereby concealing the horrors beyond.

It was only now as he stood shivering and naked on the landing that he began to grasp, albeit dimly, the enormity of what had happened.

He first stared at his arms and legs. Although they were covered in blood and a kind of yellow slime they were now thin, ordinary arms and legs. He then tentatively touched his chest and shoulders. Here too the great folds of flesh had vanished, leaving the raw torso of a very thin, naked, man. When he looked in the antique mirror in what had once been his mother's bedroom, the face that stared back at him was that of a gaunt man roughly his age but with hollow, clearly defined cheek bones, an aquiline nose and a chin and neck as lean and as finely honed as that of an athlete.

The consequences of this remarkable, somewhat miraculous transformation took a while to sink in.

After he had washed the blood and mucus from his new, angular body Antonio spent several hours staring into the long mirror in his father's bedroom. What he saw there made his spirits soar for it was clear that he now possessed the body of a thin, beautifully proportioned man. Indeed, he was almost handsome - even though his facial features were still patently his.

Antonio had been reborn. It was a modern miracle!

But first he had to clear up the mess on his bedroom floor. It was a horrible job but one that he knew had to be done, even if it took all night. He bagged the solid lumps of blubber and skin and mopped up the rest, emptying what he could down the lavatory pan.

He then disinfected the room with bleach, hung the rugs out to dry in the early morning sun on his balcony and opened all the windows and shutters to get rid of the sickly-sweet smell that now pervaded the house. Later that morning the dustmen unwittingly removed fat Antonio's remains.

For the first few days of his newfound freedom, Antonio existed in a kind of wild delirium. He took to wandering about the house dressed only in his underpants. Whenever he caught his reflection in a mirror or window he would stop, adopt the pose of a somewhat camp bodybuilder and lovingly admire his new, svelte image. Sometimes he literally jumped for joy, gyrating to some crap Italian pop song on the radio and leaping from room to room.

Since his own clothes no longer fitted him, he raided his father's wardrobe and soon reappeared before the mirror in a pin-striped suit, white shirt and collar and brown brogue shoes - the epitome of the city gent. He felt great. However, it took him a day or two to pick up courage to step outside into the streets of Porto Maurizio. While his immediate neighbours had taken little interest in the fat boy at number thirty-seven, they were still curious to know what had happened to him. He persuaded them that he was Antonio's first cousin 'Roberto' come to look after the house while Antonio went to the Villa Scassi Hospital in Genoa - to have his jaws wired together. It was hoped that this would help him lose weight.

It could, added 'Roberto' (alias Antonio), take some time!

During the next few months 'Roberto' became quite the man-about-town. He was transformed in every way and exuded a confidence and authority that he had once thought beyond him. Since none of his neighbours or (even fewer) friends ever imagined that he was the old Antonio, 'Roberto' quickly established himself as a business man to be reckoned with. He invested in stocks and shares - just as his father had done - and quickly prospered. He sold the family home, invested the money well and bought himself a posh car and a very expensive town house in the centre of Albenga. He even acquired a wife - a docile yet extremely pretty little creature whom he could easily dominate.

And there the story might have ended - the happy conclusion of an inexplicable miracle that had transformed him overnight from an obese individual into a lean, fit, powerful man oozing self-confidence and newfound authority. However, despite his wealth and apparent happiness, the anger and resentment that had clearly fuelled his dramatic transformation still seethed within.

He began to hunt down those people who, when he was fat, had made his life such a misery. At first he merely observed them from as distance, following them home from work perhaps or tracking them down in other ways - but never making direct contact. However, once he had collected a dozen or so of those whom he deemed had been cruel to him, he found ways to meet them socially. None recognised him of course. All, however, were pleased to be brought into his wealthy social orbit, even though they could not imagine why they, of all people, had been invited onto his yacht or unexpectedly chosen to attend parties at his beautiful house off the Piazza dei Leoni in the medieval heart of Albenga.

At first the changes to these people were minor but then, as weeks and months passed, Antonio's deadly influence began to emerge.

For example, the slim young girl who had once so cruelly rejected him as a teenager rapidly turned into a fat, overblown woman. She lost her figure and her looks almost overnight and became a very plump creature that even her devoted husband subsequently abandoned for a blonde, nineteen-year-old waitress from Poggi. The fellow clerk at the insurance agency in Alassio with whom Antonio had once shared a desk turned from a lean, cadaverous youth into an ugly, very fat individual who waddled to work each day and who eventually could not even squeeze into the office lift. As for the cruel geography teacher, he fell into a tub of indigo dye on a field trip to Merzougha in Morocco. Months later he turned up back at his school looking like an enormous blue balloon, much to the amusement of his class of insensitive ten-year-olds.

One by one, under Antonio's evil influence, these people grew fatter and fatter. If Antonio touched you, you were doomed. You in turn, once infected with Antonio's 'fat bug', would quickly infect others - and so on and on. It was like a plague; a plague of infectious, obese giants stalking the streets of Liguria - quickly spreading to Genoa, Milan, Rome, Nice and beyond

Soon the whole of Europe was filled with fat, ugly people.

And what about America? Could it happen there - this evil plague of fatties touched by a vengeful, irresponsible Antonio whose very breath infected innocent and guilty alike?

Who knows! Perhaps it had begun already - this irresistible spread of fat people across the globe? Soon the entire planet could collapse under the combined weight of so much human blubber.

And what if it did? Would that not leave Antonio the thinnest, most handsome man on earth. Nothing wrong with that, surely?

11
Rosie's secret

'Now spank me.'
'You what?' he replied nervously.
'Spank me. On the bum. Lots of women like it. Go on!'

This was an unexpected turn of events so for a moment or two he was not sure what he should do.

'Get on with it!' said Rosie, somewhat impatiently.

So he bent her over his knee and slapped her with the flat of his hand.

'Harder' she said. 'Much harder.'

She had turned up at his cottage one summer's evening, already fairly drunk. He was sat on the patio, enjoying the sunset and the smell of the lawn he had just cut. He topped her up with a double gin or two, whereupon she fell backwards into the bushes. He picked her up, staggered indoors and laid her on the sofa. Before he could gather breath she was on top of him, smothering him with passionate kisses and groping for his flies.

Well, one thing led to another and before you could say 'Jack Robinson' they were at it, on the living-room carpet.

And that was how it all began.

He was called Trevor. He was thirty-three and a scaffolder, although he occasionally moonlighted as a steeplejack. He had been married twice, once when he was young and more recently to a dietician who, after three years, ran off with a joiner. This really pissed him off, not least because of the stick he had to take from his mates at work. Since then he had drifted in and out of relationships in a rather desultory manner. He enjoyed his work, especially when he could display his climbing skills. He worked out at his local gym and was proud of his finely-honed body. Because of the dangerous nature of his work he was very well paid. In fact, he was in 'easy street' and at the top of his profession - literally.

For the last seven months he had been living in Cockermouth but one night some little bastard from Maryport nicked his car. The police found it three days later, smouldering on a rubbish dump near Alston. Two weeks later, at seven in the morning, he found someone else's car burning merrily in the high street - right outside Barclays Bank. That, and the street fights outside the Bull every Saturday night, were enough to persuade him that Cockermouth was not the secure, white-collar enclave generally thought but a frontier town of dubious character.

He resolved there and then to avoid towns and look for somewhere in the countryside, some rural retreat away from all this urban angst.

Being a city boy, born and bred in Preston, he had never lived in the country. He was used to the back streets and cobbled alleyways of Lancashire rather than the rolling hills and farms of Cumbria. But you never know till you try it, do you? So, he left Cockermouth at the end of the month for a rented cottage near Whippleston, on the outskirts of Blennergusset.

Whippleston and district was sheep-shagging country - as far as he could tell. Mind you, the 'sheep-shaggers' here were probably far better off than most farming folk, what with foot-and-mouth and all that compensation. You should have seen the spanking new four-wheel drives outside the village hall on those nights the Countryside Alliance held its meetings. Sure as eggs is eggs, someone made a lot of money out of the slaughter of them poor animals - and it certainly was not the local hoteliers hereabouts. Anyway, that's what Trevor thought.

The cottage itself was cosy enough, even though in the middle of nowhere. It had a lovely garden in which to sit on a summer's evening and a big log fire to warm your toes by the rest of the time. To be honest, he loved the place - even if the roads were always covered in muck and the fields stank of cow dung. That, surely, is a small price to pay for living in the countryside.

He met Rosie a day or two after he moved in. Mind you, the village was so small that it was impossible to keep anything secret, let alone the arrival of a good-looking new incomer, and a single one at that. She had smiled at him in the street, told him her name was Rosie, adding that he was always welcome at her house. She was, it turned out, the wife of a recently retired schoolmaster. He was called Vernon. Odd couple, she being a statuesque brunette in her early forties and he a thin, balding little man considerably older - but then it takes all sorts, don't you think?

After their first dramatic encounter on the carpet she visited his cottage once or twice a week, or whenever Vernon was away at one of his numerous Rotary Club events. You seldom saw Rosie and her husband together and yet they seemed close enough. She never once criticised Vernon and always spoke of him with genuine affection, or so Trevor thought. This he found rather disconcerting, never having been in an adulterous relationship before. Still, she was a real 'goer' and one should always make hay while the iron's hot, so to speak.

These stolen moments with Rosie were exhilarating but because of the clandestine nature of their affair he rather missed holding hands, candlelit dinners, walks in the park or visits together to Tesco's - all of which he considered part of ordinary, normal relationships. He had had his fair share of women but Rosie was different - not least because her idea of sexual fulfilment was a sound walloping.

After their first union on the carpet they graduated to his bedroom where she quickly proved a highly accomplished lover. Indeed, her athletic prowess was remarkable, considering her age. She was, moreover, a generous lover and always made sure that Trevor came first. If Trevor wanted her on her back, she would oblige. If Trevor wanted her standing up, so be it.

Her preferred position, however, was on top. At first Trevor found this difficult, being a bloke, but the more he did it the more she moved up and down the other end, as it were - which, all things considered, was a very satisfactory arrangement.

Trevor's favourite position was doggie-style. This Rosie enjoyed too, provided that whenever she shouted 'Ride 'em, cowboy!' he slapped her hard on the bum. This too he found difficult at first but after several weeks he got used to it and thereafter joined in the fun, slapping her as hard as he dared - considering he had never hurt a woman in his life, least of all with the flat of his horny hand.

Afterwards they would lie quietly in each other's arms for an affectionate kiss and a cuddle - until Rosie had to go home to make Vernon his tea. She and Vernon only lived a few yards up the lane, in the converted pub, so it was not as if she had far to go. What their neighbours thought of Rosie's comings and goings was anyone's guess but after a few months of the best sex he had ever had in his life Trevor started not to care either way. What will be will be, he reasoned.

He even began to enjoy the spanking - much to his surprise.

Rosie had two preferred positions. The first was kneeling on the bed with her face buried in a pillow and her shapely bottom stuck up in the air, as proud as punch. Trevor would then have to kneel behind her or slightly to one side and slap her as hard as he could with the flat of his hand. At first he found this difficult, not wanting - deep down - to hurt her but Rosie's evident enjoyment gradually won him over and after a while half-a-dozen resounding slaps invariably produced muffled squeals of delight from the pillow.

Her absolute favourite position, however, was lying across his knee. This was more difficult to achieve that one might have thought.

Trevor would first sit on the edge of the bed at a slight angle. Rosie would then position herself across his lap with her crotch carefully placed against his knee, one leg on the floor for balance and the rest of her naked body half resting on the bed, with a pillow to cuddle. This position, although somewhat precarious, ensured maximum satisfaction for all concerned. After only seven or eight solid smacks she would suddenly climax, emitting a scream of intense pleasure sufficient to thoroughly wake the village - which it probably did.

Although exciting in its way, this was still all very new to Trevor. Never once had any of his previous girl friends or either of his wives displayed Rosie's peculiar interests. He was, moreover, frankly surprised at how quickly he had accommodated her desires yet part of him - good working-class lad that he was - still found spanking repugnant. Not that he was a prude, mind you. At work he had joined in the usual chauvinistic chat but he would certainly never tell his mates what he and Rosie did in the secret of his cottage deep in the country. Sheep-shagging is one thing but spanking some gorgeous brunette four times a week is something else.

Best say nothing, eh?

One night, alone in his cottage, Trevor typed the word 'spanking' into Google. To his horror it unleashed a Pandora's Box of dubious data, much of which he definitely did *not* want to know.

He had discovered, with that one simple word, a dark labyrinthine world of depravity and deviation. I will spare you the details but things went on in the name of 'spanking' that would make your hair curl. Not that Trevor was a prude, mind you, but what he did to Rosie and what those people in black leather did to each other - well, there was no comparison whatsoever.

One thing did worry him, though. Did Vernon know of his wife's sexual peculiarities?

He had naturally assumed that Rosie sought her pleasure elsewhere because she could not get it at home. He was pretty sure he was not the first secret lover to have serviced her peculiar needs but it was very difficult to imagine Vernon putting his wife across his bony knees and spanking her until the pips squeaked.

Difficult to imagine, that is, until one day Trevor pulled down her knickers to reveal a pink bottom crisscrossed with ugly red welts.

'Good God, Rosie! What's happened to your bum?'

'Vernon.' she replied demurely, stepping out of her chemise and slipping off her bra.

'Do you mean *your* Vernon?'

'Yes, Vernon. With his belt. It was fantastic! The best yet. Now, how do you want it? On me back or doggie style?'

Soon thereafter they stopped seeing each other. Nothing was said but somehow - for Trevor, at least - the magic had gone out of their relationship.

Some weeks later Trevor met Denise. She was a nurse at Carlisle General. She was an attractive blond, about his age and with a teenage daughter from a previous relationship. After several weeks of candlelit dinners at Gianni's and walks in Bitts park Trevor quit the cottage and moved in with Denise and Kylie at their little terrace house off Warwick Road.

At first their lovemaking was rather subdued, Trevor being acutely conscious of the presence of thirteen-year-old Kylie in the room next door. Soon, however, things improved. Indeed, their little family became quite cosy - once Kylie had got used to the attention Trevor lavished on her mother. After a few weeks cohabitation and some subtle bribery to keep Kylie happy, Trevor and Denise settled into a comfortable, albeit unexciting sexual relationship.

One night - after making love in their gentle, affectionate way - Trevor asked Denise if she would like a good spanking. She gave him a horrified look, jumped out of bed and stomped off to the bathroom, slamming the door noisily behind her.

'Pity,' though Trevor and promptly fell asleep.

12
My Uncle Alf

The bullet entered her chest from above, passed through her lungs - narrowly missing her heart - and lodged in her lower spine, just above the pelvis. One might have expected the impact to have sent her crashing onto her back but instead, from a kneeling position, she fell forward, smashing her nose on the parquet floor. Stunned, and in deep shock, she now lay on her face in a pool of blood. It is Friday, 18th September, 1931.

When she came to some minutes later she felt no pain but knew instinctively that she was seriously wounded. One arm lay stretched out above her head while the other was trapped beneath her stomach. She could move her eyes but that was about all. She appeared to be paralysed.

From her position face down on the edge of the carpet she could just see her uncle, still standing above her, the gun in his hand. His face was pale and his body trembled. Suddenly, he threw the gun to the floor. It fell only inches from her face. Although she could not see it she could smell it. He then sat down heavily in an armchair opposite and stared, not at her, but into the middle distance - lost in his own thoughts.

It had all happened so quickly.

A blow to the head had sent her reeling. When she had picked herself up from the floor he was standing over her, the gun pointed at her. She raised herself onto her knees, still reeling from the blow, grabbed his hand and tried to twist the Walther 6.35 from his grip. He wrenched his hand away, stepped back and again levelled the gun at her. The abrupt explosion that followed and the sudden pain in her chest was as unexpected as it as shocking.

She cautiously opened her eyes once more. Her uncle had now vanished but she could hear him, in the hallway. He was on the telephone. Perhaps he was calling for an ambulance. She knew that her wounds were serious. The bullet had probably damaged her spinal chord for it was now clear to her that she was not only incapable of movement but unable even to speak or cry for help. She was still bleeding profusely because the pool of blood had extended from the carpet to the parquet floor. She was in danger of drowning in her own blood.

Her uncle did not return.

For several minutes she lay there, listening. Somewhere, at the far end of the large apartment a door slammed but then silence. She felt terribly alone, abandoned. Was there no one in the flat who could help her? Where was Maria their housekeeper or her uncle's servants, Georg and Anni Winter? And where was Emil, the chauffeur? He had once loved her, had he not? He cared for her, more than anyone. Where was he, now that she really needed him?

But where, above all, was her uncle?

She must have then passed out again for when she next regained consciousness there were others in the room. She could not see them but she guessed there were at least six, talking amongst themselves in whispers. She wanted to call out, to attract their attention but when she tried to speak she was unable to move either her mouth or her tongue. Instead, from deep within her damaged lungs, there came a strange, involuntary gurgle - a very dark, almost subterranean sound.

The voices continued, more agitated now. She recognised Strasser and Schwarz but the others could be any of the political thugs her uncle used. Munich was full of such people. Gentlemen of the Brown House, Maria called them. But they were not gentlemen. Even Emil, who had once regularly shared her bed, was dangerous in the way these men were dangerous. Yet, despite his brutality and coarse manners she needed him now more than ever.

She had first met Emil Maurice at a party function in Weimar, when she was just eighteen and he was twenty-nine. They first became lovers when she moved to her uncle's new flat at 16 Prinzregentenplatz.

This nine-room apartment was in a prosperous, residential quarter in Munich - far away from the student bars and cafes that, as an erstwhile medical student, she had frequented. Here, in her uncle's new residence, she had her own bedroom and bathroom at the end of the corridor, next to his. Her bedroom was painted in pastel green; there were embroidered sheets on her little bed and painted motifs on the furniture. The flat itself was very large, modern and well furnished but hardly the place for a young, vibrant girl looking for fun. Whenever she could escape, therefore, she headed for the student quarter and the bohemian temptations of Schwabing. Her uncle did not approve of these 'outings' so she kept them as secret as possible, only leaving the flat when he was away on business. The servants knew, of course.

Emil was short but stocky and very strong. When he embraced her he crushed her girlish body, like an over-affectionate bear. Although most people within her uncle's extensive household knew of their affair, she and Emil acted like secret lovers, meeting surreptitiously whenever they could.

If her uncle was away Emil would slip up to her little bedroom. He never stayed long. After making love to her he would creep away like a thief in the night, leaving her battered and bruised on the crumpled sheets. Sometimes they made love in the back of the Mercedes. Emil would park it in some secluded spot on the outskirts of Munich. Afterwards, they would drive back to the city, she seated demurely in the back with Emil, the ever-attentive chauffeur, at the wheel.

Leisurely drives in the country, stolen kisses on the landing - these and other fond memories she recalled affectionately, long after she had fallen under her uncle's devastating spell.

Her 'Uncle Alf' of course had always known of her 'secret' affair with Emil and may even have encouraged it, subconsciously. But when the couple announced that they were engaged he become so angry that Emil feared for his life.

He consequently made them promise to wait two years before marrying but she would have none of that. Later, when her relationship with the chauffeur inevitably became physical, he insisted on her telling him all the details. His salacious, far from avuncular interest in her 'secret' sex life annoyed her at first but later, as she invented more and more outrageous escapades, she began to enjoy these little tête-à-têtes. Indeed, this pornographic 'game' between uncle and niece turned them both on. Eventually her affair with Emil cooled - to be replaced by an intense, sexually charged relationship with her strange, charismatic guardian uncle.

She was now drifting in and out of consciousness with increasing regularity. As these memories of Emil came and went, so too did her awareness of what else was happening in the room. Although unable to move, she still felt the presence of five or six men nearby. Their excited, often argumentative whispers rose and fell, like a distant roar in her ears. Suddenly, two pairs of black leather boots appeared within her line of vision - two men clearly staring down at her. She tried to cry out for help but her tongue refused to move. Tears of pain and frustration in equal measure ran down her cheeks and onto her lips - she could taste the salt even though the smell of her own blood was now overwhelming.

After a while the boots disappeared, retreating to the far end of the room. The angry whispers had now stopped. A distant door slammed and then another, followed by the faraway clatter of the metal gates of their lift opening and closing and the familiar hum as it descended to street level. Dogs could be heard barking, but far away as if in some distant land. Silence then descended on the room like a shroud.

She was appalled at the callous way she had been abandoned. She knew why, of course. She had always been an embarrassment to these thugs, protective as they were of her uncle. Questions would be asked - especially by a hostile press. In their minds at least she was as good as dead. Besides, their immediate task was to get their leader out of Munich, provide some kind of alibi and explain away, as best they could, a young woman's dead body in his flat - even if it was his niece. If her uncle's bullet had not killed her, then the callous indifference of these political animals surely would.

The pool of blood had now spread across the parquet floor and was starting to disappear under the dresser but her broken nose had stopped bleeding. She closed her eyes and slowly drifted into unconsciousness once more - entering a darkness full of confused dreams. Then, out of the velvet night, there slowly emerged speckled sunlight and trees, as seen from the back of a fast moving car.

These trips to the Bavarian countryside with her uncle had been the start of their relationship. At first he had been formal towards her but her natural exuberance, her dazzling smile and good looks soon had him mooning over her like some love-sick calf. Sometimes, when he thought no one was looking, he would gaze at her longingly until he remembered and instantly assumed his normal 'Napoleonic' pose. Party members were astonished to see her on his arm, especially at official gatherings.

But these trips to the countryside, even with Emil driving, were always very special to her and her generous, adoring uncle.

Once at the lake she and her girl friends would disappear behind some bushes, disrobe and then dash into the water - amidst squeals of girlish laughter. She loved swimming naked, even if the waters of the Chiemsee were always cold and made her nipples stand up like thimbles. Afterwards, the girls, some much younger than Geli, would lie naked on the fine white sand at the water's edge, trying to get brown. One day a cluster of butterflies, fluttering gently, settled on Geli's back. The men, lounging in folding canvas chairs placed beside the cars, always watched the girls bathing and waved encouragement. They would then light their pipes and return to their politics.

Later they would all picnic at the water's edge on chicken or cheese and salami sandwiches, followed by apple tart washed down with pink champagne - all except her uncle who preferred Apollinaris mineral water. It was during their meal that the men, even the older ones, would flirt with her and her young, vivacious companions - but always discreetly, mindful of their leader's protective gaze.

Since there was now money in abundance, her uncle lavished gifts on her - Art Deco jewellery, expensive dresses, beautiful silk lingerie and even a white fox fur stole one winter. Each time he bought her a new outfit he would find an opportunity to show her off publicly. He loved opera so she often accompanied him to the first night of some new production. Always the best seats, of course. When he entered his box, large sections of the audience would stand and applaud. He would acknowledge this with a brief wave before sitting down in his stiff, formal manner. Sometimes she would wave back, basking in the reflective glory of her celebrated companion. She was still only twenty-three, after all. After the performance, when she longed to linger on the great staircase of the opera house or sip champagne in the gilded hall of mirrors with all the glamorous men and women of Munich, her uncle would whisk her away and the black Mercedes would speed off into the night.

Back at the apartment, once he had dismissed Emil and sent the servants off to bed, he would sit on the large sofa beside her and talk endlessly about the opera they had just seen - all the while caressing her knee until she relented, opened her legs and allowed him to touch the most intimate part of her young body. Although she secretly enjoyed these caresses, the clumsy urgency with which he abused her often annoyed her. Then she would push him off her and hastily retreat to her little bedroom, locking the door behind her. Later, when his knocking and whispered pleadings had stopped, she would masturbate - thereby finding the sexual fulfilment his crude foreplay always failed to kindle.

She awoke with a start, pushing these memories back into the dark, unconscious world where she knew they belonged. She tried to cry for help again but neither her lips nor her tongue responded, leaving her gasping for air like a drowning fish. Her breathing now was harsh and intermittent and all the while she could hear the distant gurgle from her damaged lungs rising to the surface as if it were some subterranean monster of the deep.

She knew now that she was dying and a great sadness overcame her - like the dark, ominous clouds that often envelop the snow-capped peak of the Watzmann, high in the Bavarian Alps. Again she slid, inexorably, into a coma of tortuous dreams and disturbed memories.

It is late one evening at the apartment when her uncle - in her nightmare - enters her bathroom, wearing only his silk dressing gown.

He has an emaciated, almost hairless chest and thin, intensely white legs. He grins sheepishly. She is naked - having just stepped out of the shower. He takes a large white towel from the rail and envelops her, wrapping his arms about her in the process. She responds warmly, letting him kiss her neck as his hands roam over her body - pretending to rub her dry. She then lets the towel drop to the wet tiles, turns to face him and kisses him hard on the mouth while pressing her body against him. Moments later he is on the floor, on his back and with his hand frantically rubbing his engorged penis.

Still naked, she at once straddles him and urinates all over his chest and belly. He comes almost immediately - with a pathetic little whimper. She stares down at him for a moment then leaves him lying on the floor like a wet rag and returns to her bedroom.

Geli awoke with a start. The telephone was now ringing. Although she could not see it she knew that it was only feet away. In the silent room it was a harsh, brutal sound. She quite expected one of the servants to come in and answer it but no one did. After a while it stopped and silence once more descended on the room like a great blanket. Geli's tears of anguish ran down her face until they merged with the congealing pool of blood that now surrounded her. The darkness returned.

In her dream there now appears a young woman with brown hair and a winsome smile. She is seventeen and very pretty. She works in a photographer's studio. In this dream she is on a ladder, reaching up for a file. Geli's uncle now appears, takes hold of her slim ankle and gazes up at the girl. She is wearing a Bavarian dirndl dress but is otherwise naked - except for white, knee-length stockings. Suddenly, we are in a large, crowded restaurant. It is the Osteria Bavaria. Geli's uncle is seated to one side, surrounded by male cronies. There is much laughter, drinking and noise. The young girl is now sitting next to him. No one is talking to her so she takes a paper napkin and writes a note on it then secretly slips it into her companion's pocket.

Geli jerks back into consciousness, remembering at once where she found that very same note - two days later, in her uncle's coat pocket.

The knowledge that he loved someone else was shattering - even though she herself was growing tired of their increasingly perverse relationship. Eva? Who is this Eva? When she challenged him, when she screamed and shouted at him he took his gun from the sitting room drawer and waved it at her, trying to calm her. Instead, she called him all the names under the sun. He started to rant, waving his arms about like some demented windmill. She laughed in his face. He struck her hard with the flat of his hand, sending her crashing to the floor. When she grabbed the gun he wrenched it free, stepped back and shot her at point blank range.

This time, however, as she relives that moment in all its vivid violence, she experiences neither pain nor the sudden impact of that fatal bullet. Instead, she feels cool, translucent water on her naked body.

She is now swimming; swimming naked in a beautiful Bavarian lake that stretches out before her. It is a warm, summer's evening and the surface shimmers with reflected light. There are, moreover, countless butterflies fluttering above her, their delicate wings gently fanning her exposed neck and shoulders.

As she swims further and further from the shore she recalls, not the sudden threat of Eva Braun, but happier days when she and her Uncle Alf basked in their own love for each other. True, theirs had been an odd relationship, even perverse but she had always loved him. There had of course been other lovers and not just Emil but they were nothing compared to the intensity and excitement of being with her extraordinary uncle.

But why had it all ended so tragically? What had she done to anger him - to such an extent that he had first struck her and then shot her at point blank range?
She had always known that he was capable of great cruelty. Indeed,

that in itself was part of his attraction to her, as with so many of his followers. But was she not different? Was his affectionate and entirely submissive young lover not his own special little girl? His little ray of sunshine in a darkening world? She had done many things for his pleasure that she sometimes felt ashamed of but then he always knew that, because she loved him, he could ask anything of her.

Is this then how he rewards her? Is this why she, of all the people close to her adored uncle, must now die?

As Geli moves effortlessly through the water, blue ripples spread out on either side of her like gentle, undulating folds of pale blue silk. She luxuriates in its soft touch and spreads her fingers wide, stroking each wave as if caressing some tactile, living creature.

It is sensual, dreamlike and very beautiful. She is happy at last.

She swims on and on into the vast blue lake until its waters merge with a white, cloudless sky at the rim of the horizon and the butterflies vanish as quietly as when they had first appeared one summer's day a long, long time ago.

The End

Footnote

If you enjoyed this book, then please let me know. I will always welcome constructive criticism and always enjoy a (brief) chat with my readers.

You can reach me by email:

Mike.healey@hotmail.com

No spam please!